W9-BGF-970

A Note from the Author:

When I first began writing, it was decided that my real name was more than a mouthful—and besides, most writers had pseudonyms. So I wrote under the name Marie Nicole. But now Silhouette has agreed to let me come out of the closet. I feel a little like Clark Kent finally revealing himself to Lois Lane: happy to get his secret out in the open at long last, but a little apprehensive as to how it will be received. At any rate, *Adieu*, Marie Nicole; hello, Marie Ferrarella (it rhymes with "Cinderella").

I'd like to take this opportunity to thank all you wonderful readers for giving me the gift of letting me know that you've enjoyed reading my stories (almost as much as I've enjoyed creating them). For me this is what it's all about: entertainment and enjoyment. I hope my stories continue to entertain you.

Sincerely,

Marie Ferrarella

Dear Reader:

The spirit of the Silhouette Romance Homecoming Celebration lives on as each month we bring you six books by continuing stars!

And we have a galaxy of stars planned for 1988. In the coming months, we're publishing romances by many of your favorite authors such as Annette Broadrick, Sondra Stanford and Brittany Young. And that's not all—during the summer, Diana Palmer presents her most engaging heroes and heroines in a trilogy that will be sure to capture your heart!

Your response to these authors and other authors of Silhouette Romances has served as a touchstone for us, and we're pleased to bring you more books with Silhouette's distinctive medley of charm, wit and—above all—romance.

I hope you enjoy this book and the many stories to come. Come home to romance—for always!

Sincerely,

Tara Hughes
Senior Editor
Silhouette Books

MARIE FERRARELLA

The Gift

Published by Silhouette Books New York

America's Publisher of Contemporary Romance

To Nicholas,
who gives new meaning
to the words "holy terror"
and who could never be contained
in a little cabin for a day,
much less four

SILHOUETTE BOOKS
300 E. 42nd St., New York, N.Y. 10017

Copyright © 1988 by Marie Rydzynski-Ferrarella

ISBN: 0-373-08588-5

First Silhouette Books printing July 1988

Printed in the U.S.A.

MARIE FERRARELLA

is a natural romance writer because her own life has been so romantic. She met her husband-to-be in tenth grade and began dating him in college. The first time he kissed her he made the room fade away, and things have only gotten better for them since.

NEVADA

THE SIERRA NEVADAS

CALIFORNIA

Pacific Ocean

Chapter One

"Mister, you've got the most beautiful fireplace I've ever seen."

He heard the words as soon as he walked in, arms laden with firewood. Saw her standing there inside his cabin, hands outstretched toward the fire. Yet for one long moment Luke Randall couldn't believe she was real.

A cold blast of wind blew his hair into his eyes and chilled his neck. He'd been so stunned by the sight of the small woman that he'd left the cabin door open. Perhaps, he thought as he turned to close the door with his shoulder, when he turned back, no one would be there and the cabin would be empty. As it should be.

But someone was there—a young woman warming herself at the flagstone hearth. She was slightly bedraggled, wet with melted snow and yet still oddly radiant.

A mirage? No, those only happened outdoors, in the desert. The Sierra Nevada was not known for mirages. And mirages didn't come with two small children, a hunched old man and what looked like a mountain of brown-and-white wet fur with legs. Luke assumed there was a head in there somewhere.

The fact of the matter was that they were trespassing, and he wanted them gone. Now. He didn't need people around; he'd gotten used to the solitude. It was what he liked, needed.

He turned his attention back to the woman. "What the hell are you doing here?"

They were not exactly the kind of words Eve would have expected to come from a savior, but because his cabin had, thank heavens, been in the right place at the right time, she forgave him. She gave him what she hoped was her friendliest smile. "Defrosting. I'm awfully sorry for barging in like this, but we had no choice. We're lost." He seemed not to hear her.

Luke realized that she was allowing herself the luxury of warming her hands, since she'd clearly already seen to the needs of the two small children who stood on either side of her. Because they were bundled in jeans and royal blue ski jackets, Luke had no idea if they were two boys or two girls or one of each. Their hair appeared to be the same length of silken flax. The children, whatever gender they were, looked so much like the nervy, animated woman. He noticed that the fire was glowing more brightly than when he had left the cabin half an hour ago. She must have added some wood. Damned presumptuous of her.

Eve watched the frown grow deeper on the man's tanned, rugged face. She got a definite impression that the small cabin contained two adversaries. But she was friendly. He was the one creating this tense atmosphere. She began to worry again.

Who was that old man? Luke wondered impatiently. The scowling gnome in the plaid hunter's jacket was sitting in his rocking chair, the only upholstered one in the cabin. Luke took a step forward, then decided that the man wasn't scowling so much as trying to steady his breathing. Luke felt a fleeting sense of concern then suppressed it. That's not your way anymore, he reminded himself. These people were strangers to him, and they were going to stay that way.

As Luke took another step forward, the mountain of wet fur came at him. Dark, glowing eyes beneath long brown-and-white shag appraised him. A low, rumbling bark resounded. Luke braced himself, the pieces of wood he'd fetched tumbling to the ground. All but one. That one Luke hefted in his hands like a crude bat.

Luke heard a sharp intake of breath and realized it came from one of the children. They both watched him, eyes wide with fear. The woman spoke.

"Whiskey won't hurt you."

"Not that I couldn't use some at this moment, but what are you talking about?"

The woman let out a deep, throaty laugh that washed over Luke and stirred something within him even as he warily kept his eye on the dog.

It felt wonderful to laugh, Eve marveled. For a few unnerving moments back there, she'd been sure she'd never laugh again, never do anything again. She'd seriously regretted the whim that had caused her to attempt to recapture a bit of her own childhood and prompted her to bring Alex and Kristin out here with her to the Inyo National Forest retreat. They'd been

here before, but never in the winter, and since they
were California children, they'd never seen snow. As
a Minnesota transplant, she decided it was high time
they sampled some. Uncle Chester had insisted on
coming with them. They were going to have an old-
fashioned Christmas. Only things hadn't exactly gone
according to plan, and though normally that made life
exciting for her, this was a little more excitement than
she'd planned on.

One look at the stranger's face told Eve that he
didn't share her sense of humor. She stifled a laugh
and pretended to cough. "Whiskey's our dog."

Luke watched her unzip her jacket. He caught sight
of a pink pullover sweater and a slight, almost boy-
ish, form beneath it. She left the warmth of the fire—
reluctantly, it seemed to him. She dug into the hope-
less tangle of fur and found her dog's collar. With a
tug, she made the animal heel. She looked like a wisp
trying to hold on to the wind, Luke mused. It looked
as though the animal had ten pounds on her at least.

"He won't hurt you," Eve said. "He just wants to
say thanks. We'd all like to say thanks." She wished
he'd say something positive.

Luke eyed the dog. The mutt could say thanks by
leaving, he thought. He gazed around the room. They
could all say it by leaving. The words hovered on his
lips, but for the moment he left them unsaid. Something from his past threatened the integrity of the armor he had forged over the past few years.

"What possessed you to bring a dog up here?" he
asked, still eyeing Whiskey.

"He's like one of the family," Eve informed him.

Luke glanced toward the old man in the chair. "I
can see some resemblance."

For Chester's sake Eve pretended she didn't catch the comment. "Because he loves the outdoors," she went on. "And because when we tried to leave Whiskey in a kennel once, he refused to eat."

The animal looked like a small horse, Luke thought wryly. "That could be seen as a blessing by some."

Definitely not the savior type, Eve thought. She stayed where she was. Outside, the wind was changing from gusty to ferocious, bringing with it clouds and snow that ripped open over the mountain area. The mournful howling intensified the loneliness that Eve sensed permeating the cabin.

Luke watched the woman, who seemed preoccupied now. Moisture glistened like a crystal halo around her face, hanging on her straight, shoulder-length hair and making her look a little like the Christmas angel his sister Teresa had chosen as her favorite decoration when he'd been young, which seemed like a hundred years ago. The memory from the past disturbed him. It had found a crack and come through, something that hadn't happened for a long time. He frowned, then bent down to pick up the wood.

"Look, lady—" he began.

"Eve. Eve Tarrington."

Fitting, he thought. Eve, second citizen of Eden. Except instead of an apple, she'd brought two kids, a grumpy man and a...thing. "Eve," he acknowledged with a slight inclination of his head. He marched over to the wood box and dumped the contents from his arms. Out of the corner of his eye he saw the old man start, then settle again. "I'm afraid you can't stay here," Luke told her.

She noticed that he hadn't given his name in exchange. She wasn't making any progress. "I'm afraid that we can't stay anywhere else," Eve said in a voice that revealed not so much self-assured confidence as a feeling that this was just the way things were. "It's snowing."

Luke brushed a layer of snow from the shoulder of his tan parka. "I noticed."

"Quite heavily." Eve looked at him a little nervously. He wouldn't throw them out—would he? Helpless females, dogs and children were supposed to get to big, strong silent types, weren't they? Hadn't he read his strong silent-type manual? She searched for an ice breaker. "It must be lonely up here for you."

He looked at her, his expression impassive. "I like the solitude."

Terrific, she thought. Her concern intensified as she looked into his dark eyes.

Each word that passed between them increased the tightness Luke felt in his chest. What the hell were these people *doing* here? he wondered again. They were staying. There was no getting around it. But they couldn't. No one had stayed in the cabin with him since he'd settled in, two years ago. He hadn't invited anyone, hadn't wanted anyone. In all that time he had never gone back, never gone away, never made use of all the vacation time he had amassed. The cabin and the surrounding area had become his adopted world. A world of peace and quiet. And he wanted it that way.

True, he thought, he did have some dealings with people. Once a month he went down the mountain to the general store at the edge of the lake and bought his supplies from Edna and Harry. And he stayed in contact with Bruce, but only because Bruce was his boss and sent him his paychecks in exchange for Luke's monitoring the weather equipment that the U.S. Weather Bureau had so carefully laid out. Bruce, Edna and Harry were the only contacts Luke had with society. He kept all three at a distance. Distance, he knew, was a state of mind more than anything else. But it would be difficult to maintain distance with five people and a dog in a living space that measured twenty-nine by forty-seven—not counting his loft.

No, they couldn't stay, no matter what the woman with the startling blue eyes said. He'd put a call in to the ranger station at the foot of the mountain and get someone to guide them down.

Without saying another word, he turned his back on Eve and walked over to the oak table in the corner. Over it were book-filled shelves that he'd made himself. On the table stood a short-wave radio, his only contact with the outside world.

He could feel her following him. Some things didn't leave you, no matter how long ago they had been learned, he thought. It was an instinct honed during his days as a policeman in Philadelphia, a long time ago, when he'd had a soul, when he had believed in the existence of one.

"What are you doing?" Eve asked, watching him warily.

"Getting you out," he answered tersely. He planted himself at the table.

Only one chair at the table, Eve thought. He really wasn't one for company. She felt exhausted, as if her legs suddenly couldn't support her. She kept what *could* have happened to her family very firmly out of her thoughts. The possibilities—no, the certainties— of what would have occurred if they hadn't found the cabin were too frightening to think about. She cast a warm look of relief at her children and then turned her face toward the cabin owner.

"We'd really appreciate that." Eve perched lightly on the edge of the table and studied him.

Who was he? What was he doing there all alone? He was clearly angry over having his solitude intruded on. There was a single, deep line on his face that ran from the bridge of his slightly crooked nose to just above his dark eyebrows. It added to his irritated look. Was he some kind of hermit? Tall, dark and decidedly handsome, with rough edges, he didn't fit the image, but then, she guessed, there might be room for clean-shaven hermits as well as bearded ones.

She watched the man fiddle with the dials on the radio, the line between his eyes growing deeper by the moment. The small, gray box was silent. Not even crackling sputters met his efforts.

"It's dead," he muttered darkly.

Watching Luke fearfully with wide blue eyes, one of the children moved cautiously until she—or he—stood next to Eve and tucked her head against her mother's arm. The woman murmured something that Luke didn't catch.

Then she told him, "And so might we have been if we hadn't found your cabin."

Eve had been about to express her gratitude more fully, but something stopped her. Instinctively she knew he wasn't the type who accepted gratitude, knew that it would make him uncomfortable. And there was enough discomfort in the cabin as it was.

She glanced around the small, barren room. There were no warm touches, no displays of personality, no pictures on the walls, no knickknacks on the mantel. It was stark, save for the books. Those gave her hope.

"You live here alone?" She knew the answer before he told her.

"If you don't mind, I'll ask the questions."

Eve shrugged indulgently, then, without conscious thought, wrapped her arms around Kristin. "Ask away."

"Thank you," he muttered. "Just what are you and the Brady Bunch doing on my doorstep?"

Eve saw Uncle Chester start to rise from his seat. He might be nearly seventy, but he was a hearty one, she mused affectionately. Had the constitution of a thirty-year-old—but the disposition of a junkyard dog when his family was threatened. She smiled, more for Chester's sake than for the man in front of her. "What we're doing is being lost. I imagine you know where you are, but, I'm embarrassed to say, *we* haven't the foggiest notion."

Luke closed his eyes. "Let me put it another way. What brought you into the forest?"

"A whim," she answered truthfully, no matter how irresponsible it might make her appear. Actually, the idea hadn't seemed so at the time. It wasn't as if they had never been at the lodge before. They had just never been there under these conditions.

Her slow answer infuriated Luke. Her smile was charming. He didn't want charming. He clung to his fury, deciding it was safer. "And this whim made you take two kids and an old man—"

"Who's an old man?" the gnome in the hunter's jacket demanded. His hamlike hands clutched the rocker's arms as he propelled himself out of the chair. That was the first thing he'd heard out of the man. Luke liked the words, and the raspy, indignant tone matched his own feelings.

Eve waved the man back into his chair. "That's just an assumption on his part. He can't see you very well, Uncle Chester. The light's dim over here." She turned back to Luke. "He's almost seventy, but he's got the spirit of a thirty-year-old."

"That's very reassuring."

The cabin owner's face was still impassive. Eve found herself wondering what he would look like if he smiled. Some smiles distorted a face, but she had a feeling that his would only enhance it.

"And just how did he and his thirty-year-old spirit, not to mention you and those two—" the man was saying.

"Kristin and Alex," she interjected amiably, nodding at each.

"And the dog—"

"Whiskey."

Luke stopped his own line of questioning, done in on all fronts by curiosity. "Why 'Whiskey'?"

"He has a weakness for it."

Luke frowned as she gave the animal a fond smile. For a woman lost on a mountaintop, he thought, she seemed to have an overabundant supply of smiles.

He rose, then braced himself against the table. "So you, Peter Pan, the Bobbsey Twins and a drunken dog decided to set out with a basket of goodies for Grandma's house and wound up here." His house was so far off the beaten path that there *was* no path. The cabin was on the mountainside, and he had chosen it purposely because visitors would have to get through the pass to get up. With very little effort these people could have met their deaths, he realized. The thought incensed him. "Don't you have any sense?"

He expected her to become angry. Instead, she looked at him with amusement.

"Why?" Eve asked, thinking of his analogy. "Are you the big bad wolf?"

He ran his hand through his hair, scattering the dark strands, making them unruly. Eve saw that the few snowflakes left there had melted. His hair was damp and brushed the edge of his collar as he moved impatiently.

"No," he said, grouchily.

She wasn't a hundred percent certain that was true. There was something slightly dangerous about him. Not dangerous in the sense that she felt her family threatened. Instead, it was just a feeling she got that there would be something entirely perilous about the man in a one-on-one situation.

She tried to look cheerful even as a strange sense of anticipation passed through her. "Well, then, there's nothing wrong, is there? I've got enough sense to get in out of the rain—and the snow."

"How did you get *into* the snow in the first place?" The man's tone was caustic. "What are you doing wandering around in a snowstorm?"

Still, Eve took no offense. In part it was her survival instinct; she knew they needed him. In part it was her nature; there was good in everyone, she believed, and she would find it in him.

"There was no snowstorm when we started out. We were just hiking." In case he had another remark, she added, "With a map. We joined up with another group of hikers from the lodge. Except they were hiking in one direction, and Alex here—" she nodded at the boy who stood off next to the old man "—hiked off in another. By the time I caught up to him, the others were far away. We couldn't find them or our way back."

"What about your map?" Luke asked.

She looked sheepish. "It blew away when the wind picked up."

"And the dog?" He nodded at Whiskey. "Why couldn't he get you back?"

Chester's deep voice rumbled at him in reply. "Whiskey couldn't find his way out of a closet."

"Somehow, it figures." Luke cast about for his options. He didn't have any. He'd have to make the best of this, like it or not. His money was on *not*.

He looked down at Eve's hand as she stroked her daughter's head. A plain gold band gleamed there. Married. Somebody else's problem as well as his.

He heard quiet sobs coming from the girl, Kristin, and felt something inside him stir. Compassion. Not his problem, he reminded himself. The world and he had parted company a long time ago, and what went on out there was none of his business.

Except that the Nordic-looking woman in the light blue ski jacket had come barging in with her brood and shoved it all under his nose.

Temporarily, he hastened to tell himself. As soon as the snow stopped, he'd guide them all down the mountain himself. Edna would know what to do about them. Even if she didn't, they'd be out of his hair and, more important, out of his cabin.

"Where's your husband?" he asked without preamble. "Shouldn't he be out looking for you?"

This time her smile was bittersweet, he noticed. Odd, the way he could almost see her think. Her oval face could be called exotic, but when she smiled, her expression was totally, guilelessly open. He saw sadness in her eyes as she said, "Not unless he's looking down."

"Is this a riddle?" he asked impatiently.

She shook her head. "My husband died three years ago."

"Oh. Sorry." Sentiment always embarrassed him. It made no difference if he was the giver or receiver. "By 'looking down,' you mean heaven, I take it."

"I mean heaven," she answered simply.

Her belief, Eve saw, seemed to disturb him. He shifted and moved back to the center of the room.

Kristin's sobs increased in intensity. "Why is she crying?" he asked a little harshly. Then he softened his voice infinitesimally as he said, "Is she hurt?" The flash of concern he felt bothered him. He wouldn't open up again, not to anyone or anything. Damn the storm for bringing them here!

"Honey, the nice man wants to know why you're crying."

Luke noticed that the woman had looked his way as she'd given him the title "nice man." He'd expected her lips to twist with sarcasm but had seen merriment in her eyes instead.

"I'll miss *Zippity Do*," came the muffled reply.

"Zippity Do?" Luke repeated. His voice sounded dumb even to his own ears.

"It's a cartoon show on Saturday mornings," Eve explained. She stroked her daughter's head and once again murmured something soothing.

Cartoons. Civilization was steamrolling its way into his life.

Today was Friday. No matter how much he had wanted to, he hadn't lost track of time in the past two years. With a shrug, he stripped off his heavy jacket and tossed it onto the sofa. Mechanically, he pushed up the sleeves of his sweater. "Well, we'll just see about getting you back in time to watch it."

He earned himself, quite unintentionally, a wide, grateful smile from the little girl. Behind him, Luke felt the hem of his sweater being tugged. Expecting to see the dog chewing on it, he instead looked down on the upturned face of Alex, the little boy. Open, just like his mother's, Luke thought. The fire had dried the boy's hair, which looked almost like platinum in the warm glow.

"Mister, what's your name?"

Giving names meant opening channels of communications, channels he had no desire to open, Luke thought. But because the boy looked so innocent, he told him.

"Are you the Luke who did all the writing?"

Luke felt himself being drawn into a conversation. He saw the old man in the rocker watching him. "The Luke who did all the writing?"

Alex pointed toward Eve. "My mom told me about him and the other three guys who wrote in the Bible."

"No," Luke said, looking at Eve over Alex's head, "I'm not that Luke, but sometimes I wish I were—he had a lot of privacy." Eve's eyes crinkled with amusement. There was something in them that tugged at Luke. He looked back at the boy.

His reply had been lost on Alex, who wasn't about to relinquish his end of the conversation. "Uh, Luke Randall?"

Luke was surprised that from somewhere within him, he could draw on patience. "Yes?"

The child stared up at him with hopeful, round eyes. "Do you have a bathroom?"

"Next to the bedroom—"

Alex ran into the back room before Luke could finish.

And with that, Luke felt his solitude slip away.

Chapter Two

Luke sighed. Eve recognized it for what it was and smiled to herself. It was a sigh of resignation.

He was letting them stay. She let out her own silent sigh of relief and exchanged glances with Chester. Kneeling, she set about working Kristin free from her parka.

Watching them, Luke ran his hand through the shock of hair that fell across his forehead. He was a man who would fight only so long against the inevitable. Besides, he wasn't a monster. To turn them out would be tantamount to signing their death warrants. Even if it weren't snowing, it was dark now. Experienced hikers had been known to lose their way in the dark, and he had a feeling she wasn't all that experienced, despite her bravado. He was stuck with them and the problem they created for the time being. He would just have to be careful not to let their presence disrupt his well-ordered life. But he had a feeling that wasn't going to be easy.

Almost unwillingly, he turned around to look at Eve. She was down on one knee, struggling to loosen the zipper on her daughter's parka. Luke shook his head and moved between them.

"It's probably frozen." He took hold of the zipper, quite unintentionally grasping Eve's fingers, as well. The fleeting contact registered with both of them. He saw a look of surprise on her face. Her eyes grew wide, as a child's will do when the unexpected happens. He tried not to notice how the light from the fireplace seemed to tangle in her hair, setting it aglow.

Eve inclined her head, encouraging him to try his luck with the recalcitrant zipper. She stood up, to give Luke more room and to place a bit of distance between them. For some reason, at this moment she felt she needed it. She rubbed her hands against her thighs. She hadn't expected him to offer any help, especially if he hadn't been asked.

It was going to work out, she thought. He was gruff, but he was definitely human. Things would be just fine. Besides, there would probably be a search party looking for them at first light.

One snap of Luke's wrist and the zipper on Kristin's jacket slid down.

Kristin stared at him, uncertainty, awe, fear all etched on her face.

"Thank you," Eve said.

The sound of her husky voice crept under his skin, he realized. He felt again the electrical spark he'd felt just seconds ago when their fingertips had touched.

He shrugged, then said, "I suppose you're hungry."

She nodded. "Famished."

Kristin's head bobbed in unison with her mother's. Luke considered his food supply and made a few mental calculations. "It figures."

His words weren't condescending, exactly, Eve thought. He just sounded as if he expected the worst from them and hadn't been disappointed so far. She wondered if he was short on food rations. Okay, Eve, she told herself, think tact.

She approached him almost cautiously just as he turned around.

"Is there a problem?"

Subtle, Eve, subtle. Keep it up and you can hand in your diplomacy badge.

They were standing toe to toe. Like two prizefighters, Luke couldn't help thinking. He looked down at Eve. He towered over her by a good twelve inches, if not more. She regarded him openly with her almond-shaped blue eyes. She made no effort to cover her curiosity about him, he mused. Standing so close to her, he became aware of just how tiny she was, compared to him. How frail. But he had a feeling that her frailty was deceptive. Nylon thread looked frail, too, until you tried to break it with your hands.

"Yes," he intoned evenly, "there's a problem." And it's you, he added silently.

Eve felt that she could almost read the words forming in Luke's mind. He was telling her that her presence there was a problem. She seized on the subject of rations instead. "I don't have to eat, but Uncle Chester and the children—"

"Don't go worrying about me," Chester chimed in, his male ego obviously bruised by the suggestion of preferential treatment.

The response was so stereotypical that Luke felt that the man had been lifted from a TV sitcom and dropped into his cabin. Luke half expected him to lumber over and put a protective arm around Eve.

"That's not the kind of problem I meant," Luke informed her.

Why did she have to be so damned pretty? And the scent that seemed to swirl around her—it was a combination of wildflowers and the outdoors. Was he beginning to hallucinate after spending too many months by himself? No, that wasn't it. She was to blame for the emotions suddenly sweeping through his mind. She brought back memories of happier times. More than that, she brought back . . . longings.

Eve was pretty sure she knew exactly what Luke meant. What she didn't know was why. Normally, people she interacted with were warm, friendly. And if they weren't that way to start with, she could cajole them into it. That was really the most important part of her job. Working with artistic types every day as a booking agent for a modeling agency, she was a whiz at soothing ruffled feathers, calming slighted egos and making fits of temperament evaporate. All she ever had to do was get to the heart of the problem. Which might not be that easy in this case, of course, she mused. Did this man even *have* a heart?

Yes, she concluded. It was just buried under concrete, that's all. Well, she loved a challenge, didn't she? And just how bearable the next few hours or more would be depended on her meeting this challenge and conquering it.

"We'll try and put you out as little as possible," she assured him. "The search party should be here in the morning."

He laughed dryly. "Not in this storm it won't be."

She conceded the point. "But it can't snow for-ever."

"No, but it'll probably be longer than either of us likes before we can make radio contact with the ranger station, and if they don't have a clue to your where-abouts, there's a hell of a lot of territory to be cov-ered. It'll be like looking for four needles in a haystack." Whiskey made a grumbling noise as he stretched himself out by the fireplace. "Five needles," Luke amended. Even the mutt was making himself at home, he thought with irritation.

Eve tried to remain calm in the face of this news. "I'll pay you for our food and lodging, Luke."

The sound of his name on her lips stirred some-thing within him, something he didn't want stirred. He'd come to terms with his life here, and he didn't want anything upsetting it. "I don't want your money, Mrs., er..."

He saw the protective look that came over the old man's face as he addressed Eve. Luke almost smiled. The man was acting true to form. Some things in na-ture didn't change.

Eve was thinking they weren't going to get any-where if they skirted around each other on a formal-name basis. "Mrs. Tarrington—but call me Eve."

Luke noticed that a dimple formed at the corner of her generous mouth. It was a mouth that seemed given to smiles and laughter. And warmth. That notion, coming out of the blue as it did, unnerved him. He usually held a tight rein on his thoughts. He *had* to, in order to keep from being haunted. This momentary slip might be an omen.

Eve was sure she noticed a flicker of discomfort pass over his face. "Then what is it you do want, Luke?" she asked softly.

He didn't like what her voice did to him.

Alex approached his mother, placed his arm around her hips and his head against her waist. He stared up at Luke, wide-eyed and expectant. Luke looked around at the crowded living area and addressed himself exclusively to Eve's question. "Space."

He was a puzzle, Eve thought, and wondered if she would get a chance to solve it. "Just as soon as the storm stops, you can point us in the right direction."

"You can count on it," he said wryly. He knew he'd have to do more than point. He'd have to lead them, but he kept that part to himself. She was the type who would take an act of unrequested kindness as a signal to become even friendlier. He wanted them all to remain strangers, nothing more.

"I had a feeling I could," she replied, sounding amused.

Eve realized that Alex was still wearing his parka. The look on her son's face as he stared covertly at Luke was one of awe. Part of it had to do with Luke's size, she guessed. Luke had to be at least six foot two. And the frame was solid muscle, if his bare forearms were any indication of the rest of him. But there seemed to be something more at work for Alex, she thought. Without a father to recall and with only Uncle Chester to relate to as a male role model, Alex was a boy in search of an idol. For his sake, she decided to bring out the best in Mr. Luke Randall while they were stranded here.

The task was not without its merits.

Eve began to undo Alex's parka. Mercifully, the
zipper slid down easily. "Now then," she continued
brightly, talking to Luke, "you mentioned food."
Alex turned in a half circle, leaving the parka hanging
in Eve's hands. She put it down on the sofa.

"In the kitchen," Luke replied.

"Good place for it."

Another quip, Luke thought. Did this woman take
everything so lightly? No, not everything. He remembered the look on her face when he'd first entered the
cabin. He'd detected a frightened look in the depths of
her eyes, despite her broad smile. He had a feeling that
Eve Tarrington, her banter notwithstanding, didn't
take all of life as a big joke.

He reminded himself that it made no difference to
him what she did as long as she did it someplace else.

Out of the corner of her eye she saw her uncle herd
Kristin and Alex over to the fireplace. As she watched
Chester struggle to get out of his jacket, she felt an-
other stab of guilt. His arthritis was acting up again.
She should never have let him insist on coming along
with them.

Eve followed Luke to the minuscule kitchen, which
contained a tiny refrigerator, a sink and stove, all
hunched closely together. The Formica countertop
that ran along in front of them, leaving a tiny area of
work space, looked totally out of place. It was difficult for all of them to move about freely in the confining space. Clearly this was meant for just one
person. The only hint that once there had been more
was the table out in the living area. It was large and
could easily accommodate Luke and her family. The
one chair that sat before it looked utterly lonely.

He'd come out to this place to be alone, Eve decided. Once again, the question *why* remained. She doubted that his retreat had anything to do with a woman. Faces like his didn't come along every day. She ought to know. Even in the high-gloss circles she traveled in, Luke Randall would be a thing apart. With its squarely cut chin and deep, penetrating blue eyes, his face might have belonged to a romanticized lumberjack. Or Superman, if the part ever needed recasting. It could have been used to launch a campaign to sell air conditioners to the Eskimos—of either gender. The women would buy because of the unconscious sensuality evident there, and the men would buy in an attempt to ape his vibrant masculinity.

So what was he doing hiding out here?

Luke turned to look back at her. She saw that there was a tiny furrow just between the perfectly shaped brows.

"I take it you were hoping for something bigger," he said.

"What?"

"The kitchen. You're scowling at it." Without thinking, he reached out and traced the tiny line between her brows. The light contact with her skin made him want more. Abruptly, he dropped his hand to his side. Maybe a little loneliness *had* set in after all this time, he thought. He had to help them get on their way as soon as possible. He didn't want to get used to anything remotely connected to the world he had left behind.

Eve tried to refocus her attention. "Oh, it's not the kitchen."

"Then what?"

"You."

Her directness brought a slight, amused smile to his sensuous lips. He's stunning, she thought.

"Do you always beat around the bush this way?"

She struggled to keep her mind on the conversation. His face was distracting her. "Bushes are nice decorations, but they do tend to get in the way of direct paths."

He watched as she shrugged out of her jacket and tossed it on the far corner of the counter. He was surprised that her slight form proved to be more amply filled out. Appealingly so. He would have been less than a man if he hadn't noticed that her small, delicate breasts stood out temptingly beneath the warm pink sweater. He felt his palms tingle. He wanted to hold her. The thought surprised him.

He made sure that when he spoke, his voice, with its edge of wry humor, masked his thoughts from her. "And what exactly is it about me that has you frowning?"

"Wondering," she corrected him. "I can't see why a man who looks like you would stay holed up in a place like this."

"What do looks have to do with it?"

"Sorry." She shrugged. "Occupational hazard."

He looked at her face. There was soft beauty beneath the dancing eyes. "What sort of occupation? Are you an actress?"

She laughed. It was a light, airy sound reminiscent of a spring breeze. She made him think of spring, spring in the midst of snow and storms. With hair like trapped sunlight.

Dangerous thoughts, Randall. You're beginning to sound like some loony old hermit. Had he reached that point?

"No, not an actress. I handle models. And you have a face that could sell anything. I don't understand what you're doing out here so far from everything."

He wasn't exactly certain how to react to her compliment and let it pass. "Maybe I just like my own company."

She cocked her head. Long blond strands brushed against her shoulder. "No, I don't think you do."

He raised a brow. "Oh, and why is that?" he asked sardonically.

She opened a cupboard and looked around. Various canned goods met her gaze. "If you did, you wouldn't scowl the way you do."

He crossed his arms in front of his chest and leaned against the edge of the counter with his hip. He couldn't help but admire her directness. He also couldn't help matching it. "Did it ever occur to you that my scowl might have nothing to do with how I view my own company but how I view yours and the invaders?" He nodded toward the threesome in the living area.

"No," she answered cheerfully. She opened another small cupboard, searching for something that resembled a pot or a pan.

Luke opened and closed his mouth, at a loss for a retort.

Eve turned her slender back toward him and bent over, determined to find something to cook with. There were cabinets built into the work counter. She flipped open their doors.

As she bent over, she brushed against his leg. Luke shivered, allowing his eyes to glide down a neat posterior in well-molded jeans.

Maybe God was testing him, he thought. A distant part of him still hung on to the beliefs of his upbringing. The beliefs were there, tethered by a slender thread that had proved too tenacious to break even after his transformation, even after he'd felt that his soul had been sucked dry of everything he had held truly dear.

If it *was* a test, this woman's intrusion far outdid a paltry plague of locusts.

"What *are* you looking for?" he asked, watching her. He dropped onto one knee and came face-to-face with her as she turned around.

"A pan..." she declared, holding up the one she had just found.

Her mouth was an inch away from his, and for a single charged moment she felt breathless. Her eyes were held captive by his, her breath refusing to move within her chest. She parted her lips as if to say something to put an end to this moment. Except that in order for her to talk, her mind would have had to be functioning. Which it wasn't.

Behind them was a welter of high- and low-pitched sounds. Chester and the children. She heard nothing clearly, except her heart beating over the rush in her ears.

Luke was suddenly aware of something he hadn't felt in a long time. He felt alive. There was a tightening in the pit of his stomach. His blood was rushing in his veins, fueling something that was now all but foreign to him: desire. He fought to control it. He didn't want to feel desire. He especially didn't want to desire a woman who invaded his inner sanctum with a brood of children in tow. He was reacting to Mary Poppins!

Yes, he was reacting all right, he realized. He wanted to kiss her more than he wanted to take his next breath. For one moment, his hand moved at his side. He was overpowered by the urge to slide his fingers across her smooth cheek.

When he gave in, he damned himself.

Eve thought she had never felt anything so tender as the touch of Luke Randall's hand. It didn't match the image of the growling man she had met just a short while ago. She suddenly felt a longing for something that had existed in her past, when she had been part of a duo, instead of a widow. She swallowed. The tension in the air was practically visible.

"I've never seen such a small kitchen." She mouthed the words, surprised to hear them. Obviously some distant part of her brain was still operating. Probably on remote control, she thought vaguely, watching his lips as he drew a fraction of an inch closer. She didn't move. She *couldn't* move.

What *is* the matter with you, Eve? This man is a stranger. When the storm is over, he'll *stay* a stranger. Why are you suddenly melting like a platter of butter in the afternoon sun?

She had no answer. All she knew was that she felt something. She wasn't altogether sure what it was, but something within Luke was calling out to her. In his own way, he needed help just as much as she and her family had when they had been lost. Lost. That was it. He was lost, too. She could see it in his eyes.

Luke carried on the thread of the conversation in order to mask his thoughts. "This kitchen was only meant for one."

"That's easy to believe."

Suddenly, Whiskey was at his side, growling. Luke dropped his hand and turned to find the dog's face level with his.

"Call off your mound of fur, Eve. I have no intention of hurting you."

Eve snapped out of her hypnotic state and was struck by the humor in the situation. It was hard to think of Whiskey as a guard dog. "I know."

Her answer, uttered without guile, intrigued him. "Oh, you do, do you?"

"Yes." Her smile softened as she regarded him, he noticed. "Those eyes don't belong to a man who would hurt me."

Why are you so sure, Eve Tarrington? What do you see there that I don't? "You have that on good authority, I take it."

"Best in the world. My instincts. They never fail."

"Oh, really?" He raised a brow, amused despite himself. "And just where were these infallible instincts of yours when you were out on the trail?"

If he meant to daunt her, he failed, she thought. "My instincts only work on people. I haven't gotten to the path-finding stage—at least not in a snowstorm."

"I see."

Was that amusement she saw in his eyes? She sorely hoped so.

When Luke rose and offered her his hand, she wrapped her fingers around it. Progress, she thought. She held on a fraction of a second longer than necessary, knowing that to an outside observer there was nothing unusual going on. But both of them, through that small act, realized that something was happening. One minuscule gesture told them both that this was the beginning of something. Neither knew quite what. Yet. For a moment each studied the other's face, looking, searching for a clue as to what the other was thinking.

"I'll take care of dinner," he informed her quietly. Whatever she had seen in his eyes was gone now, she thought a little sadly.

Eve slid her hands into her back pockets and rocked forward slightly on her toes. "We're the 'invaders,' as you called us. I don't want to put you out any more than we already have. Besides, you might like my cooking."

I don't really want to like anything about you, Eve, he told her silently. You're making things difficult already. "I might, and then again, I might not. Why take a chance on change? I prefer to stick with what I know and am comfortable with."

He wasn't talking about just food, was he? Eve thought.

Luke watched as she lifted her chin rather proudly, but he saw that her eyes held mischief in them. Some might find her irresistible, he caught himself thinking.

"You'll never know what you're missing until you try."

The look in her eyes challenged him. Her self-assurance would have normally grated on his nerves. But she spoke without a trace of arrogance, as if stating the weather conditions.

"What can you do with a can of stew?" he challenged her.

Eve was up to it. With a grin she rose on her toes, ready for the task. "If you have any seasonings, I'll show you."

He pointed to the spice rack overhead. She reached for three little glass jars. "I'm off and running."

"Ever since you came in," he muttered.

She thought it safer to ignore that for the time being. She didn't want to push her luck. "Do you have plates?"

He opened a small cupboard that was empty except for a stack of dishes—four, to be exact.

"Don't believe in overstocking, do you?" she remarked.

"I don't usually have company."

"A man like you should."

He stood his ground. If she thought she could walk in here and try to rearrange everything, she was mistaken. "A man like me doesn't want company."

"That's why you probably should have it. I think everyone needs people."

There was a hint of exasperation in his voice. Enough was enough. "Lady—"

"I'll eat out of the pot," she said quickly.

What was the source of all that humor he read in her eyes? She'd said she was a widow, had been touched by tragedy. Yet every word out of her mouth was accompanied by smiles or cheerfulness. Was she some kind of an idiot? No, he doubted that. The alternative was that she had some kind of secret to life. He envied her.

Luke walked away without a word.

Two steps from the counter and he was back amid the crowd. He needed to clear his head, but with the storm raging, there was no place to go except for the loft. He looked at the narrow wooden ladder off to the side and debated seeking refuge there. He didn't get a chance to act.

"How long's the storm going to keep up, Mr. Luke—Randall?" Alex stared up at him with a wide-eyed expression, which bespoke the fact that he regarded Luke as the power in this area, the keeper of the forest and the generator of the storm. The source of everything in this strange, frightening place. It had been a long time since he had been entrusted with such power, Luke mused. He didn't want it, yet there was nothing he could do about it.

"At least until morning," he answered.

The old man spoke up. "Get snowed in here often?" Luke couldn't discern whether he was just making idle conversation or the thought really bothered him.

"Often enough," he replied. "I usually look forward to it."

"Why?" The unusually mature voice came from the girl, Kristin. Luke looked over to where she was sitting on the floor before the fire. She looked up at him with her mother's eyes.

He could visualize Eve's eyes, he thought, stunned. Pieces of his past rushed by him. He hardened his mouth for a moment, then let his defensive feeling pass, telling himself he had no right to take it out on children. They were still young, still innocent.

So had Brian been, before he had succumbed.

Dammit, no! He wasn't going to think about Brian now. He was going to do what he had to to make these people comfortable. Then tomorrow, weather permitting, he'd scout out the pass down the mountain to make sure it was still clear. He'd take them down to the ranger station himself.

When the wind howled, his thoughts were brought back to the present. The storm was getting worse.

Well, the storms here were unpredictable. He should
know; monitoring weather conditions was what he was
getting paid for.

Kristin took him by surprise when he came out of
his state of contemplation. She stood in front of him,
staring up at his face. Everyone was studying him,
making him feel uneasy.

"Why?" Kristin asked again.

He had lost the thread of the conversation and gave
her a blank look. He saw an expression of resigned
patience cross the young face as she clarified herself.
"Why do you like to get snowed in?"

"Isn't it scary?" Alex chimed in. His blue eyes were
round beneath his blunt-cut bangs.

"Peaceful," Luke answered.

When the boy shivered, some instinct in Luke that
had been dead for two years prompted him to give
Alex a heartening smile. "Nature isn't something to be
afraid of, as long as you come to terms with it."

"Terms?"

"I stay inside. It stays outside."

Alex giggled.

Luke raised his eyes in time to catch Eve smiling
warmly at him. It was an intimate smile that caressed
him and made him feel contented. The reaction took
hold before he could squelch it.

The woman, Luke decided, was definitely dangerous.

Chapter Three

I'll do the dishes," Eve announced. The mismatched plates were all empty, and her children, she noted, looked drowsy and happy. Dinner had turned out surprisingly well, all things considered. Eve felt rather satisfied with herself.

Luke watched her as she rose from the inventively arranged table, a plate in each hand. "Certainly do know how to make yourself at home, don't you?"

She liked the way he arched one brow, even though his expression was challenging her. Everything about him challenged her. She held out the dirty plates for him. "You want to do them?"

She'd probably make a hell of a chess opponent, Luke thought. A slight smile creased his mouth. "No."

"Well, then?"

He gestured toward the sink. "Be my guest."

"That's what I'm trying to be, Luke. That's what I'm trying to be," she murmured half to herself as she turned away.

Kristin and Alex followed her closely, each carrying a plate. The dishes and pot she had used were washed and put away in short order. Eve crossed back to the oak table, which was surrounded by an odd collection of furniture in order to accommodate everyone. There were the desk chair and rocker on one side, and the sofa had been turned around from the fireplace to provide three more places. Alex had piled two pillows at the place where he'd chosen to sit.

Eve approached Luke just as he began moving the sofa back to its original position. Without asking, she placed herself on the other side of the enormous thing and began to push. Luke accepted her help without a word.

"I hate to be pushy—" she began.

His eyes met hers with an odd, half-quizzical, half-amused look. "Isn't it a little late in the evening for a personality change?"

The man was impossible, she thought as she went on. "But I think we'd better talk about sleeping arrangements."

Any other man, Eve thought, would have at least smiled suggestively at her words. Luke said nothing. His face remained emotionless as he waited for her to go on.

Eve pushed her end of the sofa over slightly until it was near the fireplace again. "You've only got one bedroom."

"Yes?"

He was going to make this difficult, too, wasn't he? Well, why should this be any different? She plumbed the depths of her being for diplomacy—she was near rock bottom. "And there's four of us."

"Five," he corrected.

His words caused her thoughts to skid to an abrupt halt. Was he talking about sleeping with them? Had she misjudged him after all? "Um..."

He liked the blush that crept up her cheek. He didn't think women blushed anymore. As a policeman he'd seen the seamier side of humanity; some young girls didn't blush. The flush in their cheeks came from drugs and alcohol.

He'd forgotten that people like Eve existed.

He decided to let her off the hook. "I meant the dog."

"Of course," she muttered, suddenly becoming preoccupied with the texture of the sofa's fabric. She ran her hand along the top, waiting for him to go on.

"I'm not having him sleep out here with me."

She looked at him hopefully. "Then...?"

"I'll take the couch. There're some extra blankets in the loft." He nodded toward the wooden stairway, really no more than a ladder, in one corner.

"I'll get them," she volunteered, and turned on her heel.

He reached out and grabbed her hand, stopping her before she could gather speed and put any distance between them. "It's my loft."

He didn't want her invading every nook and cranny of his home. He needed to keep some things safe, retain some corner, no matter how illogical the idea seemed. She couldn't be allowed to breach any more barriers.

"Right." She watched him stride past her.

"I wasn't going to steal it," she couldn't help calling after him. "My purse won't hold a loft."

He stopped, his back to her, and waited for her to finish. Randall, what've you opened your doors to? he asked himself wearily.

When she didn't go on, he went up the ladder.

End of round two, Eve thought, turning to usher Kristin and Alex into the bedroom.

At first glance the bedroom, like the living area, was stark and spartan. Except for one thing. Against the brown wood and gray stone, the bedspread stood out, a vivid splash of color. It was a patchwork quilt done in rich, vibrant hues of blue, gray and brown.

Eve reached out and touched the fabric. Soft. She smiled. A knowing, hopeful expression slipped over her face. The quilt was a hint about the inner man, the inner man she instinctively felt existed. He wouldn't have something like this here, wouldn't sleep under something like this, if he were as hardened, as remote, as he pretended to be. Her spirits were buoyed.

"You should have a good night's sleep on that," Chester observed.

Eve spun around, her thoughts scattering. It took a moment for her to take in what her uncle had said. "You're taking the bed," she informed him calmly.

Luke walked into the bedroom just as Eve and the old man were arguing. He stopped, leaning his shoulder against the doorjamb, and listened. For the moment, both parties were oblivious to him.

So Mary Poppins argues with someone other than me, eh?

Jeremiah Chesterfield's barrel chest puffed out a little with indignation. He reminded Luke of a popinjay. "I'm not letting you sleep on the floor, Eve."

Eve put a hand on his shoulder, an intimate gesture that spoke volumes. She didn't want to hurt his pride, but she was going to be firm. "Uncle Chester, I *want* to sleep on the floor."

"The hell you do," he grunted, eyeing the bare floorboards.

"It'll be like camping out, right, kids?" She turned to look down at the children.

Kristin, ever supportive of what her mother said, nodded. Alex looked rather unsure until Kristin gave him a light pinch on his arm. His eyes grew wide as he nodded in self-defense, rubbing his arm.

Chester sighed, knowing when to accept defeat. "You never did want to listen to me, even as a little girl."

"And you never wanted to listen to me, even as a maturing uncle."

He laughed despite himself. "This wouldn't have anything to do with my bad back, would it?"

She snapped her fingers, affecting a look of total surprise. "That's right. You do have a bad back, don't you?"

"All those back rubs you've been giving me for the past ten years slip your mind, girl?"

"Swept away in the storm." She leaned over and kissed his stubble-roughened cheek. "Now, be a good uncle and don't undermine my authority in front of the kids. Take the bed and make me happy." She fluttered her lashes at him coquettishly.

Chester shook his balding head. "If I were thirty years younger—"

"And not your uncle," Eve chimed in, joining his voice in the familiar, pretended lament, "you'd be a girl worth pursuing."

Eve laughed and put her arms around his neck. In her heeled boots, she was almost the same height as he was, and her arms rested easily on either side of his neck. She knew that he probably didn't look like very much to a passerby. He had a round head on an aging Pillsbury Doughboy body, and he had never been able to lay claim to the word *dapper*. But he could be described by a better word than that. He was kind. And it showed. Beneath the drooping gray mustache and the bushy steel-wool brows, the kindness shone through like a candle in the dark. "I love you, Uncle Chester."

Gruffly he brushed the sentiment aside, even though she knew it pleased him. "Yeah, I know." He smoothed his wispy mustache with two fingers and directed his glance at the children. "Okay, kids, you heard your mother. It's bedtime."

"What'll we sleep in?" Kristin lamented, looking down at her jeans and bulky peach sweater.

"Your underwear," Chester answered crisply.

Kristin looked appalled. "I'll freeze!"

"Not if the hermit has any blankets," Chester rejoined.

"The hermit has blankets."

They all turned to see Luke standing there, three extra blankets in his arms. With the two on the bed, he surmised that it gave everyone what they needed. He dropped the blankets on the foot of the bed. "There's a sleeping bag in the closet if you think the boy and girl might prefer that instead."

"My name's Alex," the boy piped up. The expression on his young face told Luke that Alex didn't like being a nonentity, even if he couldn't put his feelings into words.

"Yes," Luke acknowledged gruffly, "I know."

Eve watched as Luke turned away and walked out the door without another word. Now what? she thought.

Luke walked into the kitchenette and mechanically reached for the pot he used for coffee. There was a tightness in his chest, a tightness he tried to banish but couldn't. Watching Eve and the others interact as a family had brought back a flood of memories, memories of his life back in Philadelphia, his childhood. They were memories he no longer wanted any part of. Memories that had no place in his life now. Again he felt the rumbling of an upheaval within him, like an earthquake threatening to break everything apart, everything he had so carefully laid out. He slammed the coffeepot down on the counter.

Damn it all to hell!

Eve tucked each child into the sleeping bag, murmuring reassuring words that they had the best of both worlds: they were camping out, but they wouldn't have a bunch of insects to contend with. She kissed them and then rose to her feet. She turned toward Chester, about to speak. Her mouth closed in a smile. Steady breathing met her ear. The old man had fallen asleep in the bed. She spread a blanket over him, then put her finger to her lips as she looked back at her children. Alex's eyes had already fluttered closed. Kristin was curled in a ball next to him.

Eve's heart felt full. She was so lucky, she thought, tiptoeing out of the room. She eased the door closed behind her.

She saw Luke sitting on the couch and fought with her thoughts for a moment. Should she go back in, and leave him in peace, or approach him?

Well, what else did you come out for, Eve? To count the planks on the floor? Go talk to the man, for heaven's sake.

Despite her resolve, Eve edged her way hesitantly over toward Luke, not quite certain how he would react to her company on a one-to-one basis. Not quite certain how *she* would react to *him*.

But she wanted to find out.

She was surprised to find a mug of coffee waiting for her on the tiny wooden table before the fireplace. The mug sent up a thin stream of steam, beckoning to her like a whispered invitation. She reached for the mug, then stopped, looking at Luke questioningly.

"Go ahead." He gestured toward the mug. "It's not poisoned."

She took it in both hands. The heat felt divine. "I didn't want to be presumptuous."

"Turning over a new leaf?"

She ignored the quip and met it with one of her own. "I thought that perhaps you were a two-fisted drinker."

He met her gaze deliberately. "When I was a two-fisted drinker, it wasn't coffee I was drinking."

She wanted to ask him to elaborate, and yet something stopped her. Go slow, Eve. The man might open up if she did it slowly, harmlessly. Going in like gangbusters wasn't going to get her anywhere. She bridled her impatience, never once questioning why it seemed so important to her to *know* things about this man.

Gingerly she sat down next to him and offered a smile in return for the coffee.

"You expected me?" she asked.

"You didn't strike me as the type to just fade off into the sunset."

She laughed softly as she cradled the mug in her hands. She let the warmth ease through her palms. Then she took a sip. It was deep, rich. Wonderful.

"You make a mean cup of coffee," she observed. Nice, safe ground, Eve.

He acknowledged her compliment with a slight lift of his shoulder. For a moment she thought they were going to be doomed to silence, listening to the fire spit and crackle, unless she forced a conversation.

"You were right," he stated.

She jerked, his voice having come unexpectedly in the wake of her thoughts. "About what?" she almost stuttered.

"Your cooking. It was good."

At her grin, an image of fresh-faced pixies came to his mind. While her smile made her face almost exotic, her grin transformed it into something impish. It added an extra glow to the room.

Put a lid on it, Randall.

"Thank you. I know saying that must have been hard for you," she returned, amused.

"Oh?"

"Words don't seem to come easily to you." Not nice ones, anyway, Eve added silently.

She watched him stretch out his long, jeans-covered legs before him. He looked like a cowboy that time had forgotten about. Except time hadn't forgotten him. Time, she felt, had done something to him. Something that brought those harsh lines around his mouth and made his eyes look old.

"Out here," he drawled finally, "you learn how to use things sparingly."

The wind howled, and Eve slid a little closer to him. He was very, very conscious of her movement. Her thigh brushed against his and remained there. He tightened his grip on his nearly empty coffee mug.

Eve looked back at him, her resolve not to delve into his life being blown away by the wind. Maybe it was the situation that was giving her the courage to ask, she reasoned, although she'd never needed courage to question things before. Her question arose not from a need to challenge but from a basic, honest desire to *know*. She struggled to curb her eagerness. She had to go slowly, she warned herself again.

"How long have you been here?" she ventured.

"Two years."

Two years? Like this? A chill passed through her. "Don't you find it lonely?"

Was it her imagination, or did his slouching form before the fireplace stiffen just a little?

Luke paused, appearing to search for the right words. "I find it restful."

She took a long look around the cabin. It was sturdily constructed, not a weak chink anywhere, and stood on the mountainside like a small fortress, daring the world to break in. Just like Luke, she thought. She tried to imagine living there herself, day in and day out, without company, without voices to brighten the silent, oppressive atmosphere. A hollow feeling seized her. "Seems lonely to me."

He kept his eyes straight ahead, staring into the fire. "A person can feel lonely in a crowd."

Something in his voice caught her attention. "Were you?"

His words were deliberate, measured. They were not uttered to hurt but only to establish the barriers between them. Firmly. "That's none of your business."

"No, I don't suppose it is." She nursed her coffee for a long, contemplative moment, then took the plunge. She couldn't hold back. "*Were* you lonely in a crowd?"

He had to laugh. Stuck out here, snowed in and at his mercy, and she still didn't back off. She was either very gutsy or just this side of crazy. "You're damned persistent, you know that?"

Eve grinned into her cup as she sipped, but her eyes gave her away. "I've been told that, yes."

There was something about those eyes that pulled at him. He thought it safer looking back into the fire. Far safer. "Persistence doesn't always pay off."

Luke suddenly saw the alley, heard the gunfire once, twice, then his own, ricocheting in response. Again he saw the man's look of stunned surprise as he fell to his knees, clutching his side. A bead of sweat slid down Luke's brow as he fought to push the image back.

"Sometimes—" there was a deadly stillness in Luke's voice "—it just pays back."

She studied his profile. He seemed to have turned hard, rigid, as if there were suddenly someone else sitting on the sofa next to her. This was not the man who had offered her coffee. She wanted to know what he was thinking. "Meaning?"

He turned back toward her. The look he gave her was black. The windows to his soul were closed again. "You might get more than you bargained for."

Again she couldn't stop the words, the questions from spilling out. She had to *know*. "Did you?"

For a moment she thought she had overstepped. He took a deep breath, looking as if he were about to tell her to get the hell out of his life. Instead the breath apparently strengthened his control. When he finally spoke, it was without malice, without anger. But he was issuing a no-trespassing warning as surely as if he had just planted a six-foot sign in front of her. "That, too, is none of your business."

She knew how to back off with grace. "Not a very communicative type, are you?" she asked lightly as she swirled the remaining liquid in her mug.

"Nope."

She raised her eyes to him until her brows disappeared beneath her silvery bangs. "But honest."

"Yup." Her buoyant mood was infectious. It helped him shut away the memory she had awakened.

"And lonely." Her eyes told him that she was teasing now, not probing.

"Right now I'd like to be given the chance to be lonely."

She inclined her head and half rose. "If that's a cue..."

It should have been. He should have just let her get up and go. He had no idea what possessed him to capture her wrist and hold on to it. He wanted her to stay. Heaven only knew why.

"I don't give cues. If I want you to go, I'll say so. I'm very direct." She observed that the slightest trace of humor lifted the corners of his mouth.

"Oh?" She presented him with the most innocent look she could muster. "I hadn't noticed."

She made him want to laugh. When had he last laughed? He couldn't remember. No, no more memories! he told himself strictly.

"You're doing it again," Eve pointed out.

The woman had a way of tangling his thoughts. "What?"

"You're transforming."

He glanced down at his hands and legs, playing along with her. "Into what?"

"I'm not sure." Her voice was quiet, serious. "But twice already you've stopped to think and then the lines on your jaw tighten right there." She touched the area to further clarify her point.

The feeling of her hand on his face made a small muscle tic just beneath his eye. Leave me alone, he ordered silently. Whether he meant the thought for her or his own growing longings, he didn't know.

"You become someone cold and hard," she went on.

"Maybe I am," he answered flippantly.

"No." When she shook her head, he watched her hair shake across her shoulders. He longed to touch it. "I don't think so."

"Lady, for someone who's the new kid on the block, you certainly do have a lot of opinions on my life."

"I'm a quick study." She gave him another one of those warm, confident smiles she seemed to have in abundance. "You're keeping all your emotions locked up behind a concrete wall."

"They're better contained that way. Orderly," he stated.

"Concrete breaks up in an earthquake."

Her mental machinations began to intrigue him. "Is that how you see yourself, as an earthquake?"

She shrugged, gently setting down the empty mug in front of her. "A woman's gotta do what a woman's gotta do."

He leaned back now, an odd sort of comfort filtering through him, a feeling that had been so much a part of his life only two years ago. He laced his fingers together and cradled the back of his head. But his eyes never left her face.

"Forgive me if I'm wrong. It's been a long time for me, but isn't that sentiment out of a John Wayne movie, and didn't the line run 'A man's gotta do what a man's gotta do'?"

She was unfazed by the correction. "The women's movement has made a lot of headway in the past couple of years."

She watched as he closed his eyes and laughed. Dark lashes feathered along strong, high cheekbones. Every inch of him exuded unconscious sensuality. She could picture him at her agency. He would find himself hip deep in women in a matter of seconds. And he probably wouldn't even understand why. In a way, *he* was the innocent and she the worldly one. It was a matter of their experiences having been gathered in different worlds.

"Something tells me that I should be grateful that I retreated," he quipped. He opened his eyes to find her looking at him, her gaze unabashedly appraising.

"Something tells me that you shouldn't."

The fire's glow highlighted her lips, he saw. They were moist and tempting, and an urge, centuries old, danced through him. *Just the solitude getting to you, Randall. And she's a damned attractive woman.*

"Another opinion," he replied. "Sounds like you were bitten by a Dear Abby column as a child." He meant the words to be sarcastic but couldn't quite get his tone to match. She was disarming him. He didn't know whether to be fascinated or deeply concerned.

"I was never bitten as a child at all," she said. He held her eyes captive as she tried to read his thoughts. Nothing short of a natural catastrophe could have drawn them away. "Most animals—most *people*—like me." She shifted her gaze to his lips, then back to his eyes, and a warmth spread through her that the fire in the hearth couldn't begin to duplicate. "Why don't you?"

As if he were outside his own body, he watched his hands tangle in her hair, fingers cupping the back of her head. "Because you're an invader," he said softly, his actions belying his words.

She didn't dare move. "Why don't you refer to me as just company?"

He shook his head slowly, moving his face still closer to hers. "Too dangerous a word. *Company* usually refers to people you like."

His breath caressed her lips, and Eve felt a tightening inside. Her hands rested on his forearms, urging him on. "Would that be so bad?"

"It would be. For me." He couldn't resist the temptation any longer.

His mouth covered hers, and everything she had expected to be in his kiss faded from her mind. The touch of his lips on hers was like nothing she had ever experienced before, like nothing she had ever imagined. Could hunger, need and tenderness all be equal parts of one kiss?

Her heart hammered in her ears as she parted her lips, letting him know silently that it was all right, that she wasn't frightened—well, not completely. What she was, was utterly enthralled. She moved her hands from his forearms and lightly slid them up his back. It was such a strong back. She felt power ripple there. A woman could get lost in a man like this. As it was, she was having trouble anchoring herself to reality. He was stealing her breath away.

He wanted to hold her, to kiss each eyelid closed, to wreathe her slender throat with kisses. He felt a tightening in his loins, a cry for release. His whole body seemed to beg for it.

What the hell was he doing? Even if he could let himself go, that crusty old man or one of the children could wander out of the bedroom at any moment. Luke ended the kiss abruptly, reluctantly. How close had he come to making a mistake? A fatal mistake. How close had he come to letting her shatter his control? A bitter smile slid across his lips, which had, until a fraction of a second ago, been pressed against hers. He had a penchant for fatal mistakes, he thought.

Eve opened her eyes, struggling not to show the disappointment she felt so achingly. His was a kiss she would have gladly gotten lost in for the next century or so.

"You're very convincing," he said disparagingly. "You almost had me believing your theories about being lonely up here. I guess I got caught up in it."

Eve knew he was hiding behind that distancing humor he put up like a smoke screen when he wanted to avoid personal contact. She had to back off for the moment. Press a shell too hard and you get nothing but a squashed shell, she told herself. The soul being trapped within Luke could be set free only with patience. His kiss had told Eve that the effort was going to be worth it. There was a good man underneath all that barbed wire. She just knew it. Trouble was, she was going to have to prove it to him. Which would be hard, considering that she had no idea what had caused him to close up in the first place. But she had to try; she was already caught up in him. She had to get him to trust her. She rose and stretched, suddenly realizing how very tired she was.

Eve's simple action brought Luke's attention back to her body. What would she feel like, moving like that beneath him?

You're not going to find out, he warned himself sternly. To discover the pleasures of her body would be disastrous for him. For both of them. He was as sure of that as he was of his own character.

"Maybe I'd better turn in," she suggested.

He nodded. "Maybe you'd better." Before I do something stupid again.

But instead of taking her leave, she bent over and kissed his lips so lightly that she barely seemed to make contact at all. Except she had. The impact stayed even after she had straightened up. "Thanks for letting us stay."

He dismissed her words. "I'd do the same for any dumb creature in a storm."

"You're turning my head," she said, laughing as she walked out of the room. Luke watched as her hips swayed ever so slightly with each step she took until the door cut off his view.

He turned and swung his legs up on the couch, for the moment not even bothering to pull off his boots. He stared at the closed door. Five hours ago his life had had a deadly dull order to it that he had come to terms with. Now, suddenly, he was set upon by a band of Gypsies. And the head Gypsy threatened to undo everything he had tried so hard to do. And she was doing it rapidly.

Luke slid down on the couch and closed his eyes. If he couldn't make radio contact with the ranger station tomorrow, he was going to check out the pass

down the mountain. He'd get them down the mountain by himself, if he had to. Drastic situations war-
ranted drastic measures.

The thought, he mused as he drifted off to sleep,
was supposed to hearten him. Odd that it didn't.

Chapter Four

Eve tossed and turned restlessly on the floor, desperately seeking a comfortable position. It was useless. With all that had happened today, she had expected to drop off immediately. Instead, *because* of all that had happened today, she was wide awake and antsy.

She glanced at her wristwatch. The dim light from the fireplace illuminated its face. Five after one. She'd been trying fruitlessly to fall asleep for almost three hours. She let out a long, muffled sigh.

You're just overtired, Eve. That's what's the matter with you, she told herself.

She sat up and ran her hand through her hair, sweeping the bangs out of her eyes. She gave up fighting and surrendered. She looked at her children next to her on the floor. At least they weren't having any trouble sleeping, she thought with satisfaction. Neither was Uncle Chester, his snores proved.

With one eye on the children to be sure she wasn't disturbing them, Eve slowly stood and padded over to the window. Leaning on the cold sill, she peered out. The mournful howl of the wind had abated some time ago, but the storm hadn't. The snow continued to fall relentlessly. How long would they be buried there?

Any other cheerful thoughts, Evie?

She straightened, moved over to the fireplace and sat down there, folding her legs under her. She ran her hands up and down her arms in an effort to generate more heat than the dwindling fire was providing. That she and the others would be snowed in was a distinct possibility. She thought about the cans of food she had seen in Luke's pantry. How long would that last them? How far would they have to stretch the supplies? Would there be enough water?

Snow could always be melted down and used for drinking water, she reminded herself. Eve glanced over her shoulder at the window and the imposing sky. No fear of a shortage there.

Eve looked around the small room. There was hardly any space to move about, especially with two little bodies packed into one sleeping bag at the foot of the bed and a dog next to *that*. She rose again, picking her way carefully past the children, and then slowly opened the bedroom door. It creaked in response. She held her breath as she looked behind her. No one stirred.

Satisfied that they were all still asleep, she crept out into the living area. She wasn't quite sure what possessed her to come out. Maybe she was experiencing a touch of cabin fever.

Already, huh? You're going to be in great shape if you have to stay here a couple of days. Serves you right for wanting a white Christmas.

If she never saw snow again, it would be too soon, she thought.

Her eyes were immediately drawn to Luke, who lay on the sofa. Eve realized that she had come out hoping to find him awake. Unapproachable though he had seemed this evening, somehow his very presence gave her hope, made her feel safe. His stature had nothing to do with it. And it certainly wasn't anything he said. It was more a feeling she had about him, an aura he generated. His words to the contrary, this was a man who could keep people safe, one of the warriors of the world.

You're romanticizing, Evie.

Was she? She didn't think so. She edged closer to the sofa. He was stretched out, feet overlapping the arm of the sofa. The light from the dying fire accented his face. In sleep, his features were soft. Without his guarded look, his face held something vastly appealing. The chiseled chin didn't look quite so formidable; the creases about his mouth were gone. He looked . . . oddly vulnerable, she thought suddenly.

Who are you, really? What's your story, Luke Randall—if that's your real name? What are you hiding from? And why do I want to know so badly?

Compassion was nothing new to Eve. But more was at work here, and she knew it. There was something about Luke that prodded her curiosity. A smile came to her lips. That would be what he'd call it. Prying. But she couldn't help herself. She wanted to know about him.

Was it because she was attracted to him?

There was no denying the chemistry between them. If she'd had any doubts before about her physical reaction to him, those had vanished when he'd kissed her. She was a mature woman and had a very satisfactory five-year marriage behind her. Sexual attraction was not something that she'd just tripped over a few hours ago.

But in all her years, she had never come across the charge she felt just being in Luke's presence. There was a restless magnetism at work.

She sat in the rocking chair. It seemed so natural to be there, watching him in slumber. She remained where she was without feeling that she was intruding.

All right, Eve, what's it all about? What sort of plans are you entertaining out here alone with Grizzly Adams?

She had no ready answer.

What she did know was that she was deeply attracted to him on all levels at once: physically, mentally, emotionally. She found it a stunning reaction, to say the least. The one thing she knew for certain was that beneath his veneer of remoteness was a good, decent man. She had a sense about things like that, and she was never wrong.

Maybe what generated this romantic feeling coursing through her veins was the situation. She was rationalizing again, she admonished herself. She was sure she would have felt this attraction for him if she'd met him in the modeling agency in the midst of a dozen handsome men. It wasn't just his looks. There was something about Luke that set him apart.

Eve rocked silently for a bit. What if he woke up and found her watching him? He'd probably call her crazy. Maybe she was, just a little, she mused. Maybe she missed being married, missed the daily give and take with a man she cared for. She had liked being married, had liked having someone near her to love, to share things with, to lean on and to support in equal portions. Maybe all that was at play here were longings.

Did he have longings? she wondered. And what did he do about them when he did?

That was none of her business, just as he'd said, she scolded herself. She should just be grateful that he hadn't tossed them all out. She had to admit that two kids, an elderly man, a woman and a dog *were* a bit much to swallow.

Smiling, she recalled his initial reaction to his . . . *invaders*, as he'd termed them. She knew she should let it go at that, just accept what had happened, be grateful and stop probing. It would be over in one or two days, God willing, and then they could all go on with their lives. Separately. She and her family would return to San Diego, and he would continue his life here. Whatever it was that he *did* here . . .

More questions. No matter which way she directed her mind, questions about Luke still materialized. There was no doubt about it; she was emotionally involved, no matter *what* she told herself to the contrary. It just wasn't her way to do things in half measures. People she came in contact with, however fleetingly, became part of her. She absorbed them and they became a portion of her memories, of her life.

And Luke Randall had created quite an impression in a very short time. She knew instinctively that having come in contact with him was going to make a difference to her, would change her life somehow.

She felt a yawn coming on and stifled it with the back of her hand. Maybe now she could sleep. A calming drowsiness had taken hold of her as soon as she had admitted to herself that she *was* emotionally involved with this man with no past.

Rising carefully so as to avoid making the wooden floorboards creak, she left the chair and then made her way back to the bedroom on tiptoe.

When he heard her close the bedroom door behind her, Luke opened his eyes. He'd been awake the entire time. What had all that been about? Why had she sat here for the past ten minutes without saying a word? Not that he wasn't grateful that she hadn't tried to talk to him; he didn't want to get into another conversation with her so soon. But the whole episode wasn't like her. She was a talker.

Though he had been asleep when she'd crept out, he'd sensed her presence. His years on the force had trained him to sleep lightly, a habit he couldn't break. It was as if one ear was always open to noises that were out of place. The creak of the opening bedroom door had alerted him in his unconscious state that someone was coming out. The faint scent of her perfume had told him it was her.

At first he'd thought she'd come out to use the bathroom or get something to drink. But she'd never moved past the rocker. He had felt her eyes on him.

Had she come out to say something to him? Why hadn't she said anything, then? Her having found him asleep shouldn't have deterred her—someone else, maybe, but not her. She was the kind of person who seemed to steamroll her way through life, a participant to the nth degree. But she hadn't talked, and she hadn't gone back inside, either. She'd just sat and watched him.

She was nothing but trouble.

If he could label her so quickly, why did she make him so uneasy? Why couldn't he just shut her out, the way he'd done with everything else? After all, what was she to him? Just a nuisance, a momentary bother who would be gone within a day or two.

Get back to sleep, Randall. They'll probably be up at the crack of dawn.

Shifting to his side, he searched for a comfortable position so he could get to sleep. It was a long time in coming.

Over the age of ten, the human body was not meant to sleep on anything harder than a mattress, Eve firmly decided the next morning as she struggled to her feet. She felt as if all her joints had suddenly rusted like the Tin Man in *The Wizard of Oz*. Except in her case an oil can wasn't going to remedy the situation. Nothing short of a week in bed—a nice, soft bed— could do that.

Catching her uncle eyeing her, she forced a cheerful smile to her lips.

"Hard night?" He drew his shaggy brows together as he quizzed her.

She shook her head. "Slept like a log."

"On top of logs, you mean. Stiff?"

"Well," she said, relenting, "maybe just a little." She held her thumb and forefinger apart slightly to show him how minor the ache was. If she lied completely, he wouldn't believe her. If she told him the truth and they had to stay another night, he'd make her take the bed.

She felt torn about that. She glanced toward the window and saw the snowflakes drifting down. At least they weren't falling as if someone were vigorously shaking out feather pillows.

Chester followed her gaze to the window. "Looks like we might have to stay another night."

She took a deep breath and nodded. "I know." Mechanically she picked up her blanket from the floor and began folding it.

"That doesn't bother you, does it?" he asked.

"I was a lot more bothered yesterday when I didn't think we'd get to spend the night anywhere, ever again." She set the blanket on the end of the bed and picked up another one from the floor. She glanced at her son. "Rise and shine, sweetheart," she called to Alex.

The boy lay where he was, rubbing his eyes. "Is it Christmas yet?" he mumbled, half asleep.

She bent over him and tousled his hair. "No, it's not Christmas yet. That's still three days away."

"Oh." He shut his eyes and curled up against his sister.

Eve decided to let him stay there a few minutes longer. After all, what was the hurry? They weren't going anywhere.

"I woke up late last night," Chester said.

She turned slowly to look at him. "Oh?" Eve tried to appear nonchalant, but the simple word was pregnant with an odd sort of defensiveness that was foreign to her.

"And you were gone. Where were you?"

"Did you ever stop to think that maybe I was in the bathroom?" she countered brightly.

"You were gone a long time." He rubbed his chest in a small circle as he worriedly peered at her over his glasses. "Were you sick?"

She placed the first blanket on top of the second one. "No. Actually, I was in the other room," she answered truthfully. She wondered why she'd even attempted to lie to him. She never had before. What was the matter with her? She had nothing to hide here. The tension left her shoulders.

"I didn't hear any voices," he continued.

"That's because no one was talking."

"Then what...?"

"He was asleep," she said, pushing back the velvet bedspread and smoothing it down. The material felt good against her fingertips. She wondered if Luke's hair felt as soft to the touch.

She heard Chester reposition himself and knew he was trying to get a better look at the expression on her face. She was going out of her way to avoid his eyes, she admitted to herself. "What were you doing?" he asked.

"Sitting in the rocker and watching him sleep."

Her uncle was obviously concerned. He had raised Eve after her parents had died, and he'd been both mother and father to her for twenty years. He'd seen her through that tragedy and had held her when her husband had died. He was the closest thing to a father she had. And he knew her inside and out. "Eve—" he began.

She dropped the pillow she was fluffing. "Now, don't go taking that tone of voice with me, Uncle Chester."

"I will if it'll do any good."

She grinned impishly. "I don't know what you're talking about."

He took her chin in his hand and looked into her eyes. "You're attracted to him, aren't you?"

She shrugged slightly. "Maybe."

"Maybe?" Chester cried, then lowered his voice when he remembered that Kristin and Alex were still asleep. "Evie, you don't know anything about this man."

"He took us in," Eve pointed out.

Chester looked disgusted at her logic. "It would have been criminal not to."

"Who would have reported him?" Humor lifted the corners of her mouth.

She had him there, and she knew he didn't like it. "That's beside the point."

"That *is* the point. He's a good man, Uncle Chester, but he's been hurt."

"Is that what he told you?" he scoffed.

"He didn't have to. His eyes say it for him. He's suffered, *is* suffering," she insisted. She could just feel it.

Chester shook his head and took hold of her shoulders as if to grasp the thoughts she had before they ran away with her. "Evie honey, you can't keep trying to put Band-Aids on the world."

"This isn't the world. It's just one man."

"Who doesn't look like he wants to be bothered with a meddling female."

"I never meddle," she said, pretending to sniff. "I help."

He dropped his hands from her shoulders. Her uncle knew when he was outmatched. "You always were a sucker for an injured animal."

"Sure—look at the way I took you in," she teased him.

"You did, you know." His tone was serious.

She drew her brows together, surprised. "As I recall, I was eight at the time."

"Eight or not, you gave me something to live for, a reason to come home every night," he told her, his voice growing softer. "Eve, I don't want to see you get so tangled up that you get hurt."

She waved the notion away. "Never happen."

He gave her a dubious look. "Uh-huh." He rubbed his chest harder.

Eve watched Kristin open her eyes and smiled down at her, though her mind was still on her conversation with Chester. "You worry too much, you know."

"I have cause."

"And I have hunger," she announced, chipper now. "I'm going to see about making some breakfast. You get the kids up. See that they get their clothes on and fold their blankets."

All Chester could do was nod in response.

It was the sound of laughter that woke him. High, shrill, gleeful laughter. That and the smells of frying bacon and rich coffee. In his foggy state, he thought he was home in Philadelphia again...

Teresa was making breakfast, and Brian was complaining that it wasn't ready yet.

"Do we *always* have to wait for Luke?"

"He pays the bills; he lets us live with him. The least we can do is wait for him to come down to his own kitchen and eat with us," Teresa said once again. And Brian grumbled again good-naturedly.

But the grumblings had turned serious, and Brian had become a stranger, having grown further and further away from them.

He saw his brother huddled on his unmade bed in a room that was a shambles. Brian, who had always been so neat. Brian, the pride of the family. The baby. Brian—still, lifeless. The syringe on the floor, the hose wrapped tightly around his forearm . . .

"Brian, no!" The sob tore from his throat.

Luke sat up with a jerk, cold sweat running down his back, his face, falling into his eyes. Disoriented, he blinked as he raked his hand through his damp hair. He saw a woman standing in the kitchen, watching him. Teresa? No, his sister was back in Philadelphia. This was someone else. This was . . . Eve.

"Nightmare?" she asked softly.

He didn't want her concern, didn't want her questions. He hadn't had the dream in several months, he thought. He rose, and a shudder traveled through his body as if he were physically shucking the nightmare. "Looked that way, didn't it?"

Another nonanswer answer, Eve thought. He was good at this game, wasn't he? But didn't he ever get tired of playing it?

"What would you like for breakfast?" she asked brightly.

He went over to her, still a little dazed from his dream. He nearly tripped over Whiskey, who had suddenly gotten in the way and refused to move. "Privacy."

She pretended to ignore his grouchy tone. "That's going to be a little tough to manage, but I think the bathroom's free."

She set a mug of coffee on the counter and pushed it in his direction. "Have some—it might make you feel human."

He took it with both hands as if to fortify himself for another day with his guests. He took a long draft, letting the warmth wind through his body. Slowly he felt himself coming under control. He watched her over the rim of the mug. "Don't you ever come down off your cloud?"

She kept her hands busy with breakfast, but it was hard for her to keep her mind on what she was doing. "Could you rephrase that question, please?"

"Don't you ever get angry, upset, frustrated?"

She raised her eyes to his. "Wouldn't do any good to be that way."

"Why?"

"Why..." She pondered his question. "I don't know." She shrugged carelessly. "Maybe it's because I feel that anger isn't a productive state to be in."

"Productive?" He'd never before heard it put quite that way. He leaned against the counter and absently began to nibble the toast she'd pushed his way.

"Sure. Anger is counterproductive. Happiness isn't."

"And just what are you producing, if you don't mind my asking?"

"An atmosphere in which to survive." She buttered another piece of toast. "People live better that way, enjoy things better, enjoy one another and the world around them."

Did she actually believe what she was saying? he wondered, incredulous. "Lady, are you for real?"

"Last time I checked my birth certificate I was."

He shook his head. If she hadn't happened into his life, he never would have believed that someone like Eve Tarrington existed. She seemed to be the embodiment of oblivious happiness. "Do you know that back where I came from, people used to take drugs to get half as high as you are now?"

She merely laughed in reply. She was one of the lucky ones, and she knew it.

He contemplated his coffee for a moment, then looked back at her. "Did you stick your finger in my coffee?"

"No, of course not." She laughed. What an odd question.

He gave an exaggerated sigh of relief. "Good thing—otherwise, I might die of sugar poisoning."

"If that's a caustic remark about my personality—" she began archly.

"That's a caustic *observation* about your personality," he corrected her. So just why did he feel like smiling? he wondered.

"I'll take it as a compliment," she finished, as if he hadn't interrupted.

"You would."

When she leaned forward over the counter, her hair fell into her face. He fought an urge to push it back.

"You might be able to use a little sweetening yourself. Your perspective is all wrong. The world isn't all black, you know."

"The world I know is."

"No it's not!" Alex cried as he walked into the conversation. "It's white—all white! That's all I can see outside the window."

"That's because that's all there is at the moment," Eve answered easily. "Wash your hands and sit down at the table, honey. Breakfast will be ready in a couple of minutes.''

Alex regarded the sofa. ''But the sofa's pointing in the wrong direction.''

''Mr. Randall was just about to take care of that, weren't you?'' She looked at Luke appealingly.

''Don't have any trouble issuing orders, do you?''

''None,'' she answered blithely, turning her attention back to the stove.

Luke went to move the sofa around.

Chapter Five

Luke didn't join them for breakfast. After he'd pushed the sofa around so it faced the table, he poured himself another mug of coffee, walked over to the wooden ladder leading to the loft and placed one foot on the bottom rung. He watched them as he sipped his coffee. He made Eve think of an Indian warily watching the white man.

Indian, cowboy, lumberjack—all such solitary roles, all essentially figures from the past, she mused. Dying breeds. He created these images in her mind. There was an aura of melancholy about him, and it made her want to reach him all that much more. She had seen him smile, had seen how his face changed when he did so. He looked so much *better* that way.

But how could she reach him? she wondered as she poured another cup of coffee for Chester. She looked over toward Luke, sure he could read her thoughts. The idea didn't bother her, she realized.

She had made no effort to be coy—and wouldn't have known how. She made no pretense at hiding her interest in him, in his world, in what was troubling him. She wanted to go to him, to ask him what he was thinking about as he watched them. But the others required her immediate attention. They were polishing off their breakfasts with undue speed.

At this rate, they would eat him out of house and home by the day after tomorrow, she thought. When they got home she'd write him a check for everything they had consumed and something extra for his inconvenience.

You might not have enough money in your bank account for that, she told herself, looking back at him again. He'd already let her know that he set a high price on his privacy. For a moment their eyes met and held. She tried in vain to read the expression on his face, but it was shuttered. Maybe later, she thought.

He drained his mug and put it down on the floor next to the ladder.

Luke needed to get out. Having these people around was crowding him, crowding him far more than the reduced space would logically suggest. He was used to the cabin's confining quarters, but having these people here was making him feel claustrophobic. He had to get away from them, at least for a little while. They were jarring things in his mind that he had kept locked away for two years. The recurrence of his nightmare was all the proof he needed of that. It was time to see if the pass still lived up to its name and let him get through. With any luck, he'd have the cabin to himself again before dusk.

He glanced at the group as he crossed to the door. He wasn't feeling all that lucky.

Aware of four pairs of eyes watching him, Luke reached for his sheepskin jacket, on the lone hook on the back of the door. Five, if he counted the dog.

Eve cleared her throat. "Where are you going?"

"Out."

"Where, 'out'?"

He jammed his arms through the sleeves. Why was she questioning him? "Out the door."

Was she going to have to wrestle every word out of him? Eve thought. "Bet you must have driven your mother crazy when she tried to find out your itinerary for the evening."

Luke turned to look at Eve as he pulled the collar up high around his neck. He let a fleeting smile lift his lips. "She knew enough to give me slack."

Chester didn't look up from his plate as he spoke. "She wasn't snowed in in a cabin with you."

Luke considered the old man's words. Were they afraid he'd walk off and leave them? Well, he hadn't exactly been Mr. Hospitality, he reminded himself. He tried to put himself in their shoes. Once, that would have been all too easy to do. That had been the beginning of his downfall. He'd felt too much, bled too much. Now kindred emotions were something he wanted to avoid at all costs. "I'm going to see if the pass is clear."

"The pass?" Alex echoed.

"It leads down the mountain."

Eve watched as he pulled out a worn pair of leather gloves from the inside pocket and began putting them on.

She remembered those hands touching her hair last night. Her pulse grew erratic, and she felt a flush making its way up her cheeks. Luke was watching her as he talked. Had he noticed? If he had, he gave no indication as he continued answering Alex's question.

"If the snow hasn't blocked the trail, I can guide you all down to the ranger station, and they can take it from there."

He was eager to be rid of them, Eve thought. It looked as though she wasn't going to get the time to get to the bottom of the mystery of Luke Randall. The thought filled her with an odd mixture of sadness and loss, like an opportunity missed that could have yielded something wonderful. "If I didn't know any better, I'd say that you were trying to get rid of us," she commented.

He eyed her quietly, and she felt as if she had been physically touched. "Whatever gave you that idea?" he asked wryly.

"Paranoia?" she suggested with a lift of her brow.

It seemed odd to Luke that whenever he and Eve talked, the rest of the people around them faded into the background. "I thought perhaps you were just a good judge of character."

"If I were, I'd be able to figure yours out."

His expression grew unreadable. "Don't try, Eve," he warned. "I'm not the Jumble in the Sunday paper that you can puzzle over while sipping your morning coffee."

"That's for sure." She watched him as he put his hand on the doorknob, and an impulse swept over her. "Mind if I come with you?"

"Yes."

She was on her feet despite his answer. Flashing a smile at her uncle's quizzical look, she made a grab for the parka she'd left hanging on the bedroom doorknob. "Well, like I said," she observed as she threw the parka on, "at least you're honest."

He knew he should have walked out the door without a backward glance. Instead, he stood, watching her, amazed that she didn't take heed of anything he said. She was next to him in half a heartbeat.

"But obviously ineffectual," he said dryly. "Oh, all right, you can come."

She opened the door and stepped out into the cold. A chill ran up her spine as her body adjusted to the difference in temperature. "Coming?" she coaxed him cheerfully when he hung back, just looking at her.

Barking, the dog bounded toward the open door. "No, Whiskey, you stay here with Alex." She cast a look of appeal inside toward Chester. The man sighed heavily as he pushed himself away from the table and lumbered to his feet. He took a firm hold of the dog's collar.

"Too bad there's no way to tether you like that," Luke muttered as he shut the door behind him.

Eve merely grinned. She took a long look around. In the distance, down a slope, were fir trees dressed in huge white coats. From where she stood, they looked like toys, like the ones Chester had helped Alex arrange around his model train set last Christmas. Just before the cluster of trees was a stream, which was a mosaic of snow, ice and water. The white-gloved hand of winter was everywhere, frosting the world as far as the eye could see. Beyond that, she saw the sky, which looked dark and foreboding. Farther down the mountain, the storm appeared to be still alive and well. She remembered Luke's comment about no one looking for them during a storm. So much for a search party.

She shifted her gaze to Luke and smiled, still very grateful just to be alive and with her family. "It is beautiful out here."

He said nothing. For a moment he was too absorbed with watching the snowflakes drifting down and melting against her face and catching in her hair, like soft kisses. He realized that he wanted her, wanted her very badly. The thought materialized in his mind with an intensity he had long since forgotten. But wanting meant opening yourself up to pain. And he had sworn never to feel pain again.

Without a word, he turned his back on her and began to walk.

You're losing him, Eve, she thought as she hurried after him. Not that you ever actually had him, of course. But you were getting close. She tried again, picking a safe topic out of left field.

"How do they know that no two snowflakes are alike? I mean, how do they manage to get such a precise look before the snowflake melts?" She noticed that his pace picked up and she tried to match it. He wasn't going to get rid of her that easily. "And how can they postulate that every one *is* different? Maybe every ninth or tenth one is the same. Or every hundredth. For that matter, why—"

Luke stopped and turned around. He hadn't the faintest idea what to make of her and wasn't so sure he should even try. "Eve, if you ask me why the sky's blue, I'm going to push you into the nearest snowdrift."

She nodded slowly, the amused shine in her eyes not abating. "Succinctly put."

"I thought so." Despite his feelings about her trespassing on his life, he caught himself wanting to smile.

Luke took large strides through the freshly fallen snow. Gritting her teeth, Eve struggled to keep up with him. It didn't help matters any that they were trudging through the snow on a steeply inclined slope. She felt as if she would lose her footing any moment and go tumbling down into oblivion, gathering snow as she went until she became nothing more than a huge human snowball.

It wasn't long before she fell hopelessly behind. Luke could hear her puffing as she tried to catch up.

She cupped her mouth and called after him, "If you're trying to prove that you have longer legs, I already knew that."

He stopped and waited for her. "I didn't ask you to come along." He watched her struggle toward him and felt himself losing his battle with the smile that was steadily creeping across his face. She looked like a wobbly newborn deer, uncertain how to use all four limbs at the same time.

She shrugged, lifting her legs high to get through a particularly tall drift. "I told you, I thought you might want company."

He put his hands on his hips. "Lady, the last thing I want is company."

Who would think that something as pretty as snow would be so hard to maneuver in? she thought impatiently as she fought her way to him. With each step, the snow weighed her down more and more. Snow had seemed so much more manageable when she was a kid back in Minnesota.

"You're just saying that," she said, dismissing his answer.

"And meaning it." He was almost looking forward to her next retort now. It had been a long time since he had matched wits with anyone.

She finally caught up with him. She put one hand on his arm to brace herself and tried not to sound as breathless as she was. "What are you afraid of, Luke?"

He was aware of her touching him, even with all the layers of clothes in between. "Being driven crazy by an overly cheerful woman."

At least he didn't scowl at her when he said it, she thought heartened. "Would it help if I frowned?"

"It'd be a start," he conceded.

She dropped her hand from his arm and puckered up her face. It could have ranked as one of the world's ten most unconvincing frowns. What she accomplished was to finally get him to laugh. The sound was rich, vibrant and went to the core of her being, to be stored and treasured there. She felt almost heady with triumph. "That's nice—" she was serious for a fraction of a moment "—you should do that more often."

Luke felt almost self-conscious as he shrugged disparagingly. "Not much to laugh at out here."

They began to walk again. This time he tempered his stride to match hers. Dammit, he *did* like her company. And that would probably be his undoing, he thought.

"Then why stay here?" she asked, interrupting his angry musings.

He kept his face forward. There were too many things to be lost if he looked at her, too many secrets to be given away. "Because this is where I belong."

She shook her head, unconvinced. "Smokey the Bear belongs out here. Bambi belongs out here. People belong with other people."

He wanted her energy, her cockeyed way of seeing only the good. Was it real? Was *she* for real? "People infect other people."

She placed her hand on his arm again as if to assure herself of his attention. "Am I infecting you?"

He allowed himself one quick sweeping glance. "In more ways than you'd believe, lady."

Something in his words brightened her cheeks more than the sting of the wind. "Care to elaborate?"

"No."

"I didn't think so."

For a few minutes they walked in total silence, until she couldn't take it any longer.

"Luke, I'm worried about you. I think you've forgotten how to talk. You have the grunts down pat, but as for the rest of it . . ."

She had a way of getting to him, he admitted, of digging out smiles that filtered over his soul. He tried to suppress another one now. "Your opinions, Eve Tarrington, don't interest me."

"I don't believe you."

He sighed, wavering between impatience and a growing, strange sort of amusement. "You are the most opinionated, headstrong, tunnel-visioned person I have ever had the misfortune of meeting."

"Ah!" She held up a gloved hand as if she had just won a game point. "*Now* you're becoming more articulate."

"Do you *always* insist on seeing the bright side of everything?"

"I try to."

"Why?" She was incorrigible, he thought with a shake of his head. He began to walk again. Eve trudged after him, absently brushing away the snow-flakes that landed on her face.

"Why not?" she countered.

"I asked first."

Eve's cheeks began to feel numb as snowflakes continued to assault them. "Because it's a waste of time bemoaning what you don't have or feel deprived of."

"Sounds good to me," he muttered glibly.

She blinked, confused. "You lost me."

"No such luck." He looked over his shoulder just in time to see that her words were accidentally prophetic. She had taken a step into a drift that was too deep for her to maneuver in. Suddenly she was sinking in snow up to her hips.

"Luke!" she cried, her hands automatically reaching for his.

He lunged and made a grab for her. The sudden movement threw him off balance, and instead of rescuing her from her powdery white trap, he wound up falling on top of her, pressing her body into the drift.

He felt her quivering beneath him and thought that hypothermia had set in at a phenomenal speed. Muffled noises were vibrating against his chest. Laughter. She was laughing!

He struggled back to his feet, keeping a grip on her. She brushed away tears with the back of her gloved hand. Her whole body shook. "You'd make a heck of a Saint Bernard, you know that?"

The weight of his body had succeeded in pushing her farther into the snow. She was embedded in the drift. It took considerable effort on his part to get her standing again. When he finally managed to pull her out, her body brushed firmly against his. "You're an idiot," he declared. But the accusation was spoken fondly.

She looked up at him, ready with a playful retort, but the laughter on her lips faded. The contact between their two bodies, even through clothes, was electrifying. Suddenly the cold she had felt moments before completely vanished now as she stared up at his mouth. Her breath caught in her throat.

Neither of them was steady or ready to admit to the other reason for the sudden loss of equilibrium, even though they were both on their feet.

Aware of the rough texture of his gloves, Luke pulled one off and brushed the snow from her upturned face. The feeling of her skin beneath his fingers raised passion within him that transcended desires of the flesh. They went much deeper than that, stirred a caldron of emotions he wanted to ignore.

He was powerless to stop what was happening.

"You have snow on your lashes."

His words were barely audible. She closed her eyes and felt the soft, heart-melting sensation of his lips on first one eyelid and then the other. She moaned softly.

He trailed kisses to her cheek, then sought her lips. Needs and emotions wound tightly through him, making it difficult for him to think. They overpowered his common sense, banishing it.

What had started so gently exploded into something dangerous and powerful. Eve clung to him as if her very life depended on it. Here she had been trying to find the key to his life, trying to unlock the mysterious reasons for his self-imposed exile, and now she was discovering that she needed what he had to offer as much as she claimed he needed what she held out in her hands.

Behind his back, she ripped off her gloves. She wanted to feel his hair in her hands, wanted to touch him as much as possible. She felt him loosen the zipper of her parka, and his hands slipped in under her sweater, touching her bare skin.

She drew in her breath sharply. The cold was instantly followed by a flood of heat as his hands touched her bare midriff. She rose on her toes as he pulled her even closer. With his body pressed against hers, she felt the searing heat of his need against her abdomen.

He pressed his lips to hers, taking, giving, wanting. Her head began to swim.

Thoughts were spinning through Luke's head, as well. Dammit, this wasn't right. This wasn't supposed to happen! He had no business kissing her. Things were getting confused. He couldn't let himself give in, couldn't let himself want her this much.

With almost superhuman effort, he pushed her gently back, away from him, his breathing as shallow as hers. He looked into her surprised face. Her pupils were dilated with desire.

Why hadn't she happened into his life two and a half years ago, instead of now? If she'd been there, if she'd existed in his world then, maybe he would have been able to survive what had happened to him. Maybe it wouldn't have even happened. But now it was too late.

He released her even though what he wanted to do more than anything else in the world was hold on to her, to take her there, in the snow, and make love to her until the world ended.

He was a fool.

Annoyance at his own weakness made his features almost rigid.

"You should have stayed behind in the cabin," he told her gruffly, turning to pick up her gloves. He slapped them against the side of his leg. A flurry of snow fell from them. He held the gloves out to her.

Eve took them wordlessly, all the while watching him.

"Better yet, you should have stayed back in—Where did you come from?"

"San Diego."

"You should have stayed back in San Diego." He turned and began walking toward the mountain pass he now fervently praying was still navigable.

"Oh, I don't know," she said, striving to regulate her breathing. She pulled on her gloves as she all but trotted after him. "Everything in life happens for a purpose. Maybe I was supposed to get lost out here and stumble into your cabin."

He knew what she was insinuating. He shot Eve a dour look over his shoulder. "I'm not the one who needs rescuing, Eve. And I don't subscribe to your simplistic theory."

"That's all right, as long as one of us does."

Exasperated, he swung around. "I'm beginning to feel as if I'm some haunted individual in a Dickens novel—"

"*A Christmas Carol*?" she suggested helpfully.

"Yes, and you're the ghost of Christmas Past."

She rolled the thought over in her mind. "Never thought of myself as a ghost."

Her face was so soft, so touchingly lovely, that he felt fierce longings surfacing again. For a moment he forgot that he was struggling against her invading every facet of his life. "Angel," he amended.

This time she laughed. He could get very used to the sound of her laughter. Don't, he warned himself.

"No one's ever called me that, either," she said.

He turned his back, afraid of what she might read in his face. "My sister once had a Christmas angel that looked almost exactly like you."

"Tell me about her."

"The angel?"

"No, your sister. Did you get along with her?"

"Teresa? Yes."

"Older or younger?"

"Younger. By five years."

"Where is she now?"

"Back home."

"Which is?"

"What is this, Twenty Questions?"

She patted his arm. "Yes, and you're doing fine." There was laughter in her voice again. He rebelled against what the warm sound did to him.

"I don't want to do fine. I want you to stop asking things that are none of your business."

She gave a sigh and shook her head. "Back to that again?"

"Yes."

She pretended to pout. "And you were doing so well, too."

A dark thought flashed through his mind as he tried to curb the ray of sunshine she was causing to pierce through him. "Has anyone ever tried to strangle you?"

"You'd be the first."

"I'll keep that in mind . . . Damn."

He stopped walking so abruptly that she collided with him. "What's the matter?"

"The pass."

She looked around and saw nothing except snow and trees. "Where is it?"

"That's just it. It isn't. At least not for now." The trapped feeling came over him again. "I can't take you down the mountain."

"Oh." She digested this piece of information carefully, thinking of her children and their Christmas gifts, which were back at the lodge. "How long do these things usually last?" She gestured toward the snowed-in area.

"Sometimes a few weeks. Usually, though, it's only a few days."

At his answer, she brightened, then slipped her hand through his. "I guess you're stuck with us."

He looked at her smiling face and felt a quiver in the pit of his stomach. "Looks that way."

So why wasn't he annoyed, the way he was supposed to be?

Chapter Six

Nothing.

The gray transmitter box sat on the desk, a silent witness to the fact that the world beyond the cabin was still out of their reach. They might as well have been stranded on a desert island. When Luke had pulled the chair around and sat at the desk after dinner to try to raise someone on his short-wave radio, the room had, for exactly twenty seconds, been filled with promising noises emanating from the box. Alex and Kristin drew closer to the sound and to Luke, hope all over their faces. But then the sputtering static had stopped.

No one answered Luke's repeated calls. Kristin withdrew to a corner and resumed making her finger drawings on the frosted windowpanes. Alex didn't move. His gaze was glued to Luke's hand as if he were waiting for the man to produce a miracle.

After ten minutes of trying to regain the contact that had been his so fleetingly, Luke gave up. There was nothing to be gained by continuing. The snow was causing too much interference.

With controlled anger, Luke shut off the radio. He looked up, sensing that there were eyes on him. He assumed that Eve was watching him, but the eyes were younger. Two sets, to be exact.

Kristin, at the window, looked away, but Alex's stare was unwavering. He had been following Luke around the cabin since the latter's return earlier and looked up at the silent man now, his pale brows mingling with his straight, thick bangs.

"Nobody?" Alex asked.

"Nobody," Luke answered.

Alex pressed his lips together. Luke thought he had never seen anyone look so full of despair. He nearly reached out and touched the boy's shoulder, then stopped himself before he could offer any comfort, though the desire to do so was great. He wasn't going to continue breaking off pieces of himself for this family. He couldn't.

"Does that mean we're stuck here?" The boy's high voice cracked.

"I'm afraid so."

"Forever?"

Luke pretended he didn't see the boy's lower lip tremble. It would probably only embarrass Alex, he rationalized. As it was, the situation was embarrassing Luke. He fought the urge to gather the small body into his arms and offer words of hope. No one so young should look so sad.

It was a trap, Luke's mind warned. He couldn't fall for it, couldn't allow himself to get tangled up in people's lives again. Nothing good ever came of it, not for him and not for them.

"No, not forever," he told the boy, his voice distant. "Nothing lasts forever."

"That's nice to know," Eve said from across the room.

Luke looked over to find an enigmatic smile on her face. It was directed at him. Eve was a good name for her, he decided. Eve had caused Adam to lose Eden. And this Eve was seriously threatening his Eden, his paradise. She had a definitely perverse effect on him every time he looked at her. And he didn't like it at all. He also had no idea what her comment meant, but he instinctively knew there was something more beneath the words, something he didn't understand. He didn't like things he couldn't understand or control. That was why he was here.

Luke placed his palms flat on either side of the transmitter and pushed himself away from the desk. "The temperature's dropping again," he announced as he rose. "I'd better bring in some more firewood for tonight."

He strode to the door. Unable to keep his eyes away from her, he looked back to see Eve's mouth open as he reached for his jacket. Oh, no, not again, you don't, he told her silently. "Alone."

The single word rang through the room like a royal decree.

Eve curtsied behind the short kitchen counter and dipped her head slightly. "Yes, Your Majesty." She let one side of her mouth rise higher than the other. Her smile wasn't meant to mock him. It was intended to show him what he sounded like. She was hoping she could rouse him out of the emotional paralysis that seemed to be consuming him. She was sure that his gruffness hid something, some hurt, and that beneath it all he was a kind and gentle man. Like the man who had kissed her in the snow today.

Luke swept his gaze over Eve's face before he turned away. Damned impertinent, Luke thought as he pulled up his collar and walked out. Didn't she ever get angry? Didn't she ever shout? What was wrong with her?

What was wrong with him?

The image of her mouth stayed with him as he walked out into the dark, cold winter night. How he wanted to kiss that mouth. If only to keep it still, he told himself as an afterthought.

He was powerless to stop the smile that reached his lips. Moreover, he didn't really want to.

The temperature *was* dropping rapidly, even though the snow flurries had ceased late that afternoon. He made his way around to the back of the cabin, where he had stacked the cords of wood just yesterday morning. Before the siege, he thought with a sigh.

The woman, he decided as he hefted logs into his arms, was nothing short of a witch. He remembered a story his mother had once read to him. It warned of witches, who could take all shapes and forms.

Luke stood still for a moment, letting his mind wander back in time. His own thoughts caught him by surprise. His mother. He hadn't thought about his mother in so long. What was more, the old, familiar bittersweet pain didn't wash over him as he summoned an image of the woman whose life had touched his all too briefly. His mother, he knew instantly, would have approved of Eve Tarrington.

Well, she might, but he didn't. Not barging into his life, anyway. Her very presence was dangerous to him. And to her. He'd come up here to be alone for specific reasons. Having her here was blurring those reasons, blurring everything except the longing that he felt.

Luke set about getting the rest of the wood into the house, muttering to himself and trying to cast out unbidden images of a small, laughing-eyed woman with hair the color of platinum and a mouth that begged to be kissed.

"I don't *know* if Santa Claus will be able to find us. I guess so," Kristin answered helplessly as Alex asked her the same question for the third time in five minutes.

At the age of seven, Kristin was torn between wanting to believe that once a year a man in a fur-trimmed red suit got into a sleigh behind a team of reindeer and flew around the world, giving gifts to good boys and girls, and feeling that maybe the idea of someone, even a magical elf, doing such a hard job was too unbelievable.

Alex's growing panic about being passed over by Santa Claus was not easy for Kristin to handle. She was worried herself. She turned toward her uncle, who sat by the window. "Why don't you go ask Uncle Chester?" she prompted her brother impatiently, waving him away. "He's so old, he knows everything."

"He's asleep," Alex complained as he drew near the bulky figure in the rocker. He saw that his uncle's chin was resting against his chest and his eyes were shut, shaded by huge, shaggy brows. His glasses had slipped down to the tip of his nose, and his hands were clasped loosely on his rounded belly. Alex turned on his heel and shuffled over toward the kitchenette.

"Mom?"

Eve was slowly wiping the dishes, preoccupied with thoughts of the man who was gathering firewood outside the cabin. She blinked to clear her mind. "Yes?"

"Is Uncle Chester related to Santa Claus?"

The question took her by surprise. For a moment she was speechless. She was proud of herself for not allowing the laugh that bubbled in her throat to escape. Instead she pulled her features into a solemn expression, as if she were pondering the question. "Not that I know of."

"Oh."

She watched the eager look leave Alex's face as his shoulders sagged. "Why?" she pressed.

"Oh, nothing."

Her son's tone was sad and wistful, and Eve wanted to know why, but she stopped herself. She couldn't constantly pry into everyone's life. He was undoubtedly worried about being stuck here for Christmas. Or maybe it had something to do with whatever he and Kristin had been discussing. In any event, he'd tell her when he was ready.

She glanced at her wristwatch. And if he wasn't ready in half an hour, she'd drag it out of him, she promised herself as she began to put away the dishes.

The cold blast of air let her know that Luke was back. She shivered and felt warm at the same time. Odd how quickly she found herself responding to his very presence. She would have laughed if anyone had told her she'd be acting this way with some mountain man who appeared just as eager to see them buried up to their necks in snow as to keep them out of it.

Truth is stranger than fiction, Evie, she mused.

The memory of their last encounter, in the snow, suddenly burst on her and infiltrated every nerve ending. She wanted the pink color to leave her cheeks before he saw it, so in order to keep her back to him, she deliberately put the dishes away one at a time.

She was also suddenly having other thoughts—private, wonderful, luscious thoughts. The kind she hadn't had since before her husband had died.

Eve was glad Uncle Chester was dozing in the rocker and the children were off at the other end of the room. She didn't need questions at this moment.

Luke, she knew, might look at her oddly, but heaven knew he wouldn't pry. On second thought, he would probably be quite content to have her back toward him for the duration of their stay, she surmised. And then again, she thought, recalling his kiss, maybe not . . .

She heard the dull thud of the wood being dropped by the fireplace and then his sure steps as he strode farther away from her.

He was climbing to the loft. Why? Had he decided to spend the night there, instead of on the sofa? And, since she was spending the night in the bedroom, why did the thought fill her with such sadness?

Because she wanted the opportunity to talk to him alone again, to hear the sound of his voice and nothing else, that's why, she admitted. She was on dangerous ground. But she already knew that.

The wooden slats creaked beneath his boots as Luke made his way up the ladder. The light from below filtered up into the dusty area, which ran the length of the cabin. One lone window added to the illumination of the loft, which was crammed with things that had belonged to the previous owner, things that Luke had never really given much time or attention to. He seldom went up there. It was only five-and-a-half feet high. Had he built it himself, he would have added at least a foot to the height.

Absently Luke thought that someday he had to get around to raising the roof and enlarging the loft. As he moved around, hunched over, he felt like some sort of early martyr. The image brought a self-mocking smile to his lips. He sifted through the contents of the closest carton. Where was that last damned blanket, anyway?

A muffled sound startled him. He tilted his head slightly and listened. It wasn't coming from downstairs.

He realized that it was coming from over by the window at the same time that he made out Alex's slight form huddled in the corner, next to another pile of boxes.

His first impulse was to leave the boy alone and go back downstairs.

No, that was his second impulse, he forced himself to admit. His first, his very first, if he was honest with himself, was to find out what was wrong.

He went with his first impulse, deliberately ignoring a voice inside his head that warned him not to.

"Alex?"

There was a deep sniffle, followed by a cough. "Yeah?" Alex didn't turn in Luke's direction.

"Something bothering you?"

"No."

The lie was too much for the slight shoulders, and they shook. Without thinking, Luke picked him up and held him. He didn't look down at the boy's face.

Alex's tears were his own, even at his tender age. Everyone deserved some measure of privacy.

"If you lie, your nose'll grow."

There was a deep sniffle and then a disgusted sigh. "That's just a fairy tale."

"I wouldn't put it to the test if I were you. This cabin's already filled to capacity. You let that thing grow—" Luke slid his finger down the boy's nose "—and I'm going to have to put you outside."

When there was nothing but silence, Luke looked down at Alex. The boy was regarding him uncertainly. He obviously thought Luke was serious.

My God, Luke thought with a sigh, the kid's got me pegged as an ogre.

As much as he wanted to be left alone, the thought that he sent fear into a little boy's heart did *not* please him. It left an ugly taste in his mouth—a familiar taste.

"Are you that afraid of me, Alex?"

"I'm not afraid of you," Alex insisted immediately. He shifted away from Luke. "Men aren't supposed to be afraid."

"Says who?" Luke could see that his words thoroughly surprised Alex. "Anyone who isn't afraid under certain conditions is a fool."

Alex looked at him. His expression showed Luke that he was unconvinced. "Bet *you* were never afraid."

Luke leveled a gaze at Alex, wondering if he had ever been so trusting as a child. With a twinge of bitterness, he remembered Brian. Brian had been that trusting, that innocent.

He swallowed the bitterness that came to him. This wasn't the time or the place. "If you're planning on

winning that bet, you're going to be disappointed."
He paused, weighing his next move. An instinct that
he thought long dead took him there. "Now why don't
you tell me what you were crying about."

"He won't come here," Alex said in a small voice.

"Who won't come here?"

"Santa Claus."

Luke let out a breath. Okay, how should he handle
this one? Gingerly, he answered himself. "What
makes you so sure?"

"Then he does?" Alex's eyes grew large with hope.

Again those eyes reminded Luke of a larger pair, a
pair that unsettled him and threatened to wreak havoc
on his life. He forced himself to shut out the thought.

"Does he?" Alex pressed, looking so hopeful that
Luke found it difficult to say anything that would wipe
the look away.

"Does who what?"

"Aren't you listening to me?" Alex asked, shifting
impatiently. "Does Santa Claus ever come here?"

Luke heard a soft noise behind him and knew that
she was there with them.

He should have handed the kid over to her and let
her take care of it. Instead he heard himself answering, "Yes, he's been known to, a time or two."

He turned and saw a look of relief on Eve's face that
mirrored the one on her son's.

"Past your bedtime, young man." She held out her
hand to Alex.

Luke noticed that *she* was standing up. The loft was
made for midgets, he decided. And short pains in the
neck.

Alex went obediently. Over her son's head, Eve mouthed thank you to Luke. He lifted his shoulder slightly in response.

"He's gonna come, Kristin," Alex announced excitedly to his sister as Eve tucked him into the sleeping bag beside the little girl. "Santa Claus is gonna come. Luke Randall said so."

"Uh-huh," Kristin answered, more than half asleep. Chester was already asleep in the bed.

Alex smiled dreamily at his mother. "It's going to be all right." It wasn't a question; *he* was assuring *her*. His eyes drifted closed.

Eve bit her lower lip. She didn't want Alex holding on to promises that couldn't be fulfilled, and there weren't many things in the cabin that could pass as gifts. Yet she couldn't help smiling as she thought of Luke's lie. He was coming around, just as she had hoped he would.

Eve zipped the sleeping bag closed, rocked back on her heels and then stood. Whiskey was all set to follow her back into the other room. "No, you stay here and keep them warm, Whiskey."

The dog lay down and stretched out his huge front paws. She bent over and scratched him behind his ear. "Good boy."

She found Luke sitting on the sofa in front of the fireplace, just as he had the night before. She was half afraid to look down at the coffee table, afraid because she wanted to see the coffee mug there again, bearing a silent invitation. Afraid because she thought that this time it wouldn't be there.

It was there. She let out a sigh.

Without bothering to look up, Luke knew she was smiling. The woman was *always* smiling. He'd had half a mind to stay up in the loft, out of her way. But it was cold up there. Much, much colder.

"You're a fraud, Luke Randall."

"Top of the evening to you, too," he murmured sarcastically. What right did she have, coming in here with her brood, stirring things up and driving him crazy? Just who the hell did she think she was? He tried to nurse his anger until it took, like a small spark being fanned into a flame. But it wasn't working.

"No, I'm serious." Eve sat down on the sofa near him, tucking one foot beneath her. She picked up the mug and hugged it to her chest, savoring the warmth.

He felt a stab of desire. He wanted his hands to be there instead of the mug, wanted to inch his fingertips along that soft, delicate area until he had memorized every curve.

Her eyes were speaking to him as much as her mouth was. "You don't fool me. You're just as vulnerable as the rest of us."

He looked back into the fire and took a long drink. Finally he spoke. "Never said I wasn't."

She shrugged, undaunted. "Maybe it was the Superman cape flapping in the wind behind your back that confused me."

"Lady, Superman volunteers. If you recall, I didn't volunteer for this tour of duty."

"Not in so many words..." She let her voice trail off significantly.

"Not in *any* words." He gave her a long, hard look. "I think you're getting cabin fever." And I'm getting another kind of fever entirely, he added silently.

Why was it that she seemed more enticing each time he looked at her? he wondered. Devoid of makeup, wearing the same clothes now for two days in a row, wasn't she supposed to look rather disheveled? Dowdy? Or at least not so damned glowing and appealing? It just proved she was damned perverse about everything, he thought.

"Besides," he snapped, more annoyed with his own reactions than with her, "you don't know anything about me. You can't make any of your Pollyanna judgments."

Why was he fighting so hard to keep his barriers up? Why couldn't he just let them fall, let her in? "I don't have to have a whole detailed history of your past to know the kind of person you are."

The nearness of her was beginning to infiltrate his senses. He wanted to touch her hair, saw himself holding her in his arms. He realized that he almost wished her words were true, that she could know him for what he had been and not what he had become. The daily despair, the lusterless eyes he had encountered, the empty, broken lives that had made up his everyday life when he had been on the force had robbed him of hope, had seeped into his essence until there had been no trace of the idealistic thoughts that had made him want to take up the shield in the first place. And then the final incident had blown everything else apart.

"So you are part witch, are you?"

The way he said it told her that this wasn't the first time he had considered the description for her.

"No." Her voice was seductively soft. She leaned forward. Long, delicate fingers touched his face, touched his soul. "I just have the ability to read people rather well."

He looked at her defiantly. "And what do you read when you look at me?" He knew he should have tabled this discussion, but he couldn't quite disentangle himself. Or maybe he didn't want to, he thought.

"I see a person who's been through a lot—"

"In the past two days—" he finished for her.

"Who's been hurt." She saw his jaw tighten. "You asked," she pointed out.

He drew back, leaning against the sofa. "I won't make that mistake again."

"What other mistakes have you made, Luke?" Her voice was coaxing.

"Letting you stay."

"No, I mean really."

He tried to sound firm. "So do I." He shifted to face her squarely.

Eve thought he looked strong, unapproachable, yet somehow he had the look of a hero about him, a reluctant hero, a man whom people sought in a crowd and made their leader. A man who made you feel protected. He couldn't erase that, no matter how hard he tried, he thought.

"If I hadn't let you stay, you wouldn't be doing this to me now," he was saying.

"What am I doing, Luke?" she prodded him softly, her body leaning into his. "What?"

Her face was inches from his. He clenched his hands, telling himself that he didn't want her, that he didn't want to take her into his arms. That all this was just the work of his damned hormones.

But it wasn't lust that was in his heart. It was need, need for a woman, for *this* particular woman.

She was changing him as certainly as if she were some goddess on Mount Olympus, playing with the life of one of her people. A goddess, half Venus, half—who was the goddess of whimsy? he wondered. Was there a goddess of whimsy? If there wasn't, he nominated Eve.

He was afraid, he admitted reluctantly. He didn't want things to change. He had come to terms with his existence here. Confusion took hold.

He wanted to push her away.

He wanted to reach out and hold her, wanted to gather her to him and have her make him forget everything but her. She reminded him of when he'd been idealistic, when he'd been enthusiastic about life and about the difference he had hoped he could make in the world.

But that was a lifetime ago.

Eve was thinking, if the mountain won't come to Mohammed, she'd have to help a little. She took Luke's hands and put them firmly around her waist.

"What are you doing?" he asked.

"Positioning you," she replied.

Her eyes held mischief, but he could see the pulse in her throat jumping.

"For what?"

She tilted her head, her eyes fluttering shut as she leaned forward. "For this." She lightly brushed her lips against his.

It was all the contact he needed to make him break his resolve. Her sharp intake of breath shattered the last of his control. He tightened his hands about her waist and pulled her to him. Her soft breasts pressed against his hard chest, exploding needs within him. An ache took hold of him, far outreaching the fire in his loins.

Eve slid her hands up his back, gathering his sweater into her fists as if to anchor herself to something as his lips parted hers. She felt the sure, hot sweep of his tongue as it plunged into sweet secrets of her mouth. Excitement roared through her veins. Her breathing had grown shallow. She'd never been reduced to this quaking mass of anticipation with just a kiss.

But it wasn't just a kiss. It was everything. He made love to her with his mouth, pressing it against hers over and over again, drawing her sweetness from her as if it offered him life. As if he were a dying man seeking to cling to life just a bit longer.

Eve trailed her fingertips through his dark, shaggy hair, reveling in the silken texture. In another part of her mind, as she relished the sensations, the tastes, the smells, which all came to her at once, she came to a sudden realization that was startling and yet wasn't so startling. Somehow she had almost known all along.

She was in love with this man. He had touched her soul. He had filled the need she had for loving a man.

When their lips parted, she moaned involuntarily and then pressed her flushed face against his chest, clutching the front of his sweater for support. She didn't want him to pull away yet. Not until he understood what she understood.

Luke allowed his hand to gently tangle in her hair.

"I *know* you're a good man, Luke," she murmured softly against his chest. "I couldn't care about someone who didn't deserve it."

Her words burned against his skin.

Luke stopped stroking her hair. Reality stormed in like a cold blast of air. She said she cared about him.

He couldn't let himself believe that. Couldn't let her feel that. She didn't *know*.

"How can you say something like that?" he asked harshly. "You've only been here two days."

She looked up at him, her eyes brimming with love. The image tore at him. "I could have said it," she answered quietly as she rose to her feet, "in the first few hours I was here."

Eve smiled at him as she lightly touched his cheek. "Remember, I make up my mind quickly."

With that she turned around slowly and walked into the bedroom.

Luke stared at the doorway long after she had disappeared through it. The woman was crazy, he told himself.

But that didn't change anything.

Chapter Seven

So what is it that you do here, Luke?'' They were re-tracing yesterday's path for another look at the condition of the pass, the only reasonable route down the mountain.

The area was bright and picturesque, like a quaint winter wonderland in a Currier and Ives Christmas card. Icicles hung from tree branches like diamond earrings, capturing the sun within their prisms. The isolation that pervaded the wooded area added to its beauty, Eve thought. She could understand why a person would want to come here, to commune with nature, to get in touch with his thoughts. What she couldn't understand was why someone would want to remain here indefinitely.

She looked at Luke. His profile did not look as for-bidding as it had the first time she'd seen him. Was she responsible for that? Had she made some small dif-ference in his life? She hoped so. There was far more at stake than a simple desire to help. She had invited herself along again. Except that this time, she found that Luke resisted the idea less than yesterday.

"Keep to myself, mostly," Luke teased her, answering her question. He was softening toward her, he realized. He discovered he liked, God help him, the way she isolated the positive elements of everything about him, about everything he said—positive features he'd thought he'd lost. He hadn't been very kind to her since she arrived, yet she took it in stride—not like a fearful, docile puppy but like someone who immediately understood that there was a problem and knew that she'd have to forgive him his transgressions. She was sensitive but strong; was forceful when necessary but always coated her words with honey. He suddenly realized what he was thinking. It sounded as if he was in love with her, he thought with a flash of cynicism. Of course he wasn't. He couldn't love anyone anymore.

What would it feel like when she was gone?

It would feel like hell, he knew, but he was used to that, had dwelt with it for two years. Hell was where his soul had sunk to, where it belonged. He deserved no better for what he had become. He certainly didn't deserve someone like Eve.

Yet there, during the Christmas season, he felt that somehow he'd been granted a special dispensation, however temporary. It was almost enough to make him believe in miracles again. Almost.

But for the moment, things that had happened to him back on Twenty-third Street, on the South Side of Philadelphia, were light-years away. And nothing else seemed to exist in the world but the smile of this too-good-to-be-true woman.

Eve was aware that he was studying her. "Why are you looking at me like that?"

"I'm trying to decide whether you're real or some sort of a mirage."

Eve laughed and tucked her arm through his. To her complete pleasure, he didn't stiffen. He let her arm stay where it was. "I'm not a mirage, and you're trying to change the subject."

"Sorry." They both knew he wasn't, but it didn't matter. "What was the subject?"

"I was trying to find out what you do out here—when you're *not* keeping to yourself."

They stopped before the same tiny cabin that they'd come to yesterday. Yesterday she hadn't asked him what the assembly line of monitors were all for. She had picked her questions carefully. Today, having lived with the man for twenty-four more hours, she felt she could broach the subject.

"What *is* all this?" She gestured at the very intimidating-looking equipment as they walked into the weather-tight structure. The tiny cabin was filled to capacity with things that she could only vaguely label as scientific, but that was all she could tell. "You're obviously monitoring something. You're not just a hermit."

Luke stopped before an imposing machine that rivaled him in height and appeared to be all gauges and buttons. He wrote something down, taking his first reading. He glanced over his shoulder at her. "Are you so sure of that?"

Something in his tone almost stopped her, but she pressed on. "Hermits don't monitor fancy equipment like this."

He turned to his work. "Now you're an expert on hermits?" For once his sarcasm was laced with amusement.

She stood next to him, staring at the machine. "What is it?"

"A radiosonde transmitter and receiver."

She pursed her lips in an exaggerated expression of enlightenment. "Oh."

He laughed at her reaction. "It monitors a rubber balloon I send up once a day to measure moisture, air pressure and the temperature. That thing over there—" he pointed behind her to what looked like a converted printer "—graphs the information picked up from the anemometer on the roof."

Eve merely nodded. She appreciated his telling her what he was doing, but she had no interest in the equipment, only in the man who was making notes on their digital readouts. She thought back to his comment about her being an expert and felt that that, more than the tour on weather instrumentation, deserved an answer. She didn't want him getting the wrong impression about her. "I'm not an expert on hermits," she said quietly. "I'm not an expert on anything—except, perhaps, on hurting."

He didn't want to look at her, didn't want to respond to her. He didn't like what the thought of her hurting did to him. He'd gotten too close, after he'd sworn not to. Fighting to keep his voice even, he asked, "Oh, and why is that?"

There was no accusation in her tone, no bitterness. "Because I've done enough of it myself."

He studied her, trying to envision what her delicate, merry face would look like wreathed in sadness.

"When?" Why are you asking? his mind demanded. The more you know, the closer you get.

Eve looked out through the lone window in the cabin, keeping her mind distant from the reality of her words. She saw something moving in the snow. A deer foraging for food. Poor thing, she thought, wishing she had something to give it. She needed that separation from her thoughts. "When my parents died."

She'd caught him up as surely as if he'd stepped into a steel-jawed trap. He couldn't make himself stop probing. "How old were you?"

Eve looked away from the animal and its plight. Her crystal-blue eyes held his. "Ten. Old enough to understand that they were gone; not old enough to understand why."

Luke went back to his readouts. He made a few more notations. It helped fabricate a barrier, however slim, between himself and her, between himself and what he was feeling. Tentacles of compassion wound through him. Finally he spoke. "I don't think anyone's ever old enough to understand why."

She conceded the point with a slight inclination of her head. "All right, not old enough to come to terms with the fact."

He had to know. "How did you come to terms with it?"

"Uncle Chester."

Her answer seemed remarkable to him. "That old man?" He couldn't picture Chester doing anything but sitting off in a corner, spinning stories and frowning.

She smiled fondly. Luke liked the way her eyes crinkled into the smile. "That old man was everything I had at one point. He was my father's older brother. He took me in after my parents died. He picked up all my pieces and put me back together again when he didn't have to."

Eve shook her head, remembering how she'd been, remembering the patient nurturing her wounded spirit had required. Chester didn't have to trouble himself with her. But he had, bless him. "If it hadn't been for him, I wouldn't have been able to face Shawn's death, either."

The soft way she uttered the name brought a prickly feeling to the pit of his stomach. "Shawn?"

"My husband."

Unexpectedly a strong feeling of jealousy took hold of Luke. The idea seemed ludicrous, but he couldn't stop himself. He was jealous of a man he had never seen, had never known. A man who had held her, made love to her, who had fathered her children. A man who had shared things with her that Luke could never share.

He envied the dead man.

Luke moved on to the next monitor, mechanically making more notations in his spring binder, his mind elsewhere. Finally he asked in a flat voice, "How did he die, your husband?"

"In a light plane. Shawn loved to fly. He was kind of like you in a way."

Luke resented the comparison. "Oh?"

"He liked to reach out and touch the skies, to commune with nature."

"I'm not communing with nature," he said tersely, hating himself for his tone of voice. "I'm trying to read it."

Eve peered up at his face, then back down at the machine that supposedly held his interest. "You're a scientist?"

"Nothing as fancy as that. I'm monitoring weather equipment."

"You're a weatherman?" She raised her hand to her mouth but was unsuccessful in stifling her laugh.

He jerked his head in her direction. Already an unbidden smile was forming in response to her reaction. "Why is that so funny?"

She waved her hand at him. He didn't know which she was trying to wave away: her laughter or his accusation that she was laughing. "I always pictured weathermen as short guys in loud suits who kept dart boards in their offices and periodically sailed one onto the board to see what tomorrow's weather might be."

Luke tried hard not to let his grin show. "Very scientific."

She shrugged. "Probably just as accurate."

He couldn't help it. "Probably." He shoved his pen back down deep into his coat pocket. "Tell me something, Eve." As he spoke, he took a large balloon equipped with a small instrument package and filled it with hydrogen.

"Anything."

He lifted a brow. "It isn't wise to leave yourself so wide open." With a twist of his wrist, he secured the balloon.

"I'm not afraid," she told him quietly.

He paused in what he was doing. "Maybe you should be."

"Of you? Never." Her trust in him made him uncomfortable, she could tell. But there was no denying the fact. She trusted him. He made her feel as if nothing could harm her, as long as he was near. He made her feel safer than she had in a long time. She let the topic drop. "You were about to ask . . . ?"

He walked outside with the balloon and released it. They both watched it climb high into the sky.

"Do you find everything funny?" he asked finally.

You can't understand that, can you? she thought, aching for him. "I try to find the humor in everything, yes, or at least the good." She shaded her eyes, looking up. "How high does that thing go?"

"Oh, sometimes seventy-five thousand feet."

She moved closer to him, sensing that his work for the day was done. "Laughter is a great way to release tears, you know."

"Huh?" He carefully locked the shack door. Dropping the key into his pocket, he began to walk back to the other cabin. Slowly. He didn't want to lose her, at least not at the moment.

Eve tried to put her feet into his prints. He was a big man, she marveled. "Ever laugh so hard that you had tears in your eyes?"

"No."

She looked down at the snow, then at his back, making a quick calculation. "I didn't think so." She twisted her lips, thinking. If she stood on her toes and flung—"You should try it someday." She quickly gathered a big wad of snow into her hands. "It's a great release." With a sudden movement, she managed to dump snow down the back of his shirt.

Luke spun around with a startled yelp and dropped his notebook in the snow. "What the . . . ?"

She darted back, away from him and sought the dubious protection of a tree. She tacitly challenged Luke to take pursuit. He charged after her. Eve ran, but she was no match for him. He tackled her, sending her tumbling into the snow. Straddling her, he washed her face with a huge handful of snow as she laughed and fought, trying to buck him off.

"Mercy!" she cried. Snow fell into her mouth, and she twisted her head to spit it out. She nearly choked, laughing.

"None given."

"Rat!"

He gave her another faceful of snow. This time some slid down the neck of her sweater. She shrieked when it touched her skin. "Stop, stop! Enough!" She was laughing so hard that she shook all over, moving from side to side under him.

He trounced her with one last, hastily created snowball. And then suddenly he was laughing with her, laughing as if he hadn't a single care in the world, as if he were a kid again.

The mirth slowly dissipated. Luke became aware of the fact that she had stopped squirming beneath him. Instead she was studying him. She propped herself up with one elbow.

"See?" she asked with a satisfied smile. "You just proved my point. Laughter's wonderful therapy."

He was about to give her a flippant answer but stopped. As if all his senses had suddenly been drawn into a throbbing awareness, he realized his position over her. His legs straddled her hips. They were touching. Intimately.

She read the look in his eyes. She was still smiling at him, but now it was different, a soft, loving smile. The desire that heated his body met a twin within hers. Unmindful of the cold, of anything around her, she fitted her shoulders back into the imprint she had made in the snow and raised her hands to him.

His body covered hers as his lips touched her mouth. There was nothing soft and tender in this kiss, nothing hesitant. He took and took and took until he thought she would be drained. But she always had more to give. Her sudden flare of passion surprised him. Could her laughter, her impish ways, mask something so raw, so basic, so powerful?

He'd removed his gloves earlier in order to write, and she hadn't given him time to put them back on before she had thrown snow down his back. Now he slid his hands under her parka, delving under her sweater, exploring her silky skin. He felt her quiver and wondered if it was from the cold or if she was re-acting to him.

His fingers were drawn to the hard, tight bud of her nipples, straining against her bra. He rubbed his thumb against them over and over until she moaned and twisted beneath him. He moved his lips more urgently over hers. He wanted her more than he'd ever wanted anything. She reminded him of all that he missed, all that he needed. All he'd wanted once. She was sweet and pure, and she made him feel whole again. If only he could pretend, just for a little while—

But that was all it would be—pretending. The dark thought splintered the light she radiated into his life and brought him back to his senses.

Luke shifted slightly and supported his weight on his elbows, which were sinking into the snow. "You're going to freeze to death," he said.

"You, too."

"Might be worth it."

He kissed her and felt her smile spread beneath his lips as she murmured, "Might be."

She was delectable enough to eat.

He had no right to do this.

Reluctantly he got off her and sat up. His jeans were soaked through. One look at her told him hers were in the same condition. All of her was. "I'd better get you back to the cabin and into a hot shower before you wind up with pneumonia."

She detected a slight change in his voice and recognized it for what it was. He was trying to put distance between them. She'd almost succeeded in blasting away his armor, but it was still holding together. She had to try harder.

At the mention of a hot shower, she suddenly had an image of both of them taking the shower together. Although it was unique for her, the thought didn't surprise Eve. Nothing about her reactions around Luke surprised her now. It all seemed so natural, so right. Why couldn't he see it?

"We'd better go back and find my notebook before it disappears in the snow." He rose and extended his hand to her.

Before she took it, she stripped off her own glove. Then she reached up and wound her fingers around his hand. He looked at her questioningly.

"There're way too many things getting in our way all the time," she explained.

He nodded. He knew it would be too dangerous to talk. He hadn't been prepared to open up as much as he had to her. How had she managed to do that? How had she found the cracks within his walls and seeped in like that? She had been there less than three days, and already she'd turned him inside out, had made him long for her, had made him remember long-forgotten memories. No, not forgotten—just buried, the way he had been. The way he was, he amended.

But his Freudian slip stuck with him on the road back to the cabin.

"My God, what happened to you two?" Chester boomed when they walked in through the doorway. He stopped in midsentence. He'd been telling the children a story.

Eve smiled innocently as she pulled off her wet parka. It made a slapping noise as it fell to the floor. "I fell."

Chester looked at her suspiciously, then cast a scathing look at Luke. Luke judiciously kept his back to the old man as he took off his own soaked jacket and draped it over the coffee table in front of the fire.

"Into what?" Chester asked.

Eve gave an involuntary shiver. The warmth in the cabin contrasted sharply with how wet she felt. "A snowdrift. Luke tried to grab me. I pulled him in by accident." She pushed her wet bangs out of her eyes.

Eve watched Chester. He only pulled his mouth tighter for a moment, gnawing at his bottom lip from the inside. Chester knew she didn't have accidents and that whatever had happened out there had happened by specific design—her design.

Luke was beginning to come to the same conclusions independently. He turned to see the old man's eyes on him. He wasn't one to be stared down, Luke concluded. The whole family was unnerving. He shifted his attention to Eve.

"You'd better get to that shower," he suggested, motioning toward the tiny room off the bedroom.

"There's no point to it. I don't have any dry clothes." She looked down at her drenched apparel. Her sweater was molded to her like a second skin.

Luke felt his mouth grow dry. He forced himself to think of something besides the way her sweater accented every curve. With deliberate motions he picked up her parka and spread it out next to his. "I'll dry your clothes by the fire. I can lend you some of mine until yours are ready to wear."

Merriment touched her face as she considered the difference in their sizes. But the idea of wearing his clothes made her feel warm all over. Warm and secure. "Sounds perfect."

"Mom, can we go outside?" Alex asked, shifting from foot to foot. Longing was etched on his face. The look was duplicated on Kristin's. They hadn't been outside since they had walked into the cabin.

"Please, Mom? We're tired of drawing pictures on the window. We've been in this old cabin *forever*," Kristin moaned.

"Well," Eve hesitated, looking at Alex. She'd nearly lost him once and was afraid to risk it again. Alex had no fear of the unknown.

As if reading her mind, Chester turned to pick up his jacket from the sofa. "I'll go with them," he volunteered. "The story was getting dull, anyway."

"I want you to stay close to the cabin," Eve warned. "All of you." She looked pointedly at Alex.

"Don't have to tell me twice," Chester muttered, shrugging into his huge plaid jacket. "Mind your mother, kids. Not two steps farther than I can see you. You got that?"

"We got it, Uncle Chester," Alex called out. He'd pulled open the door and was gone in thirty seconds. Kristin was on his heels. They left the door wide open.

"Slow down, you two!" Chester hollered. He looked back over his shoulder just before he closed the door. "Don't worry about them, Evie. And get out of those clothes. I've got enough to keep my mind busy without worrying about you catching your death of cold because you were out there making angels in the snow."

The door slammed in his wake.

Eve let out a laugh that brought Luke's attention back to her in full. "He knows," she said.

He could occupy his hands with spreading out a drenched parka for only so long. He gave up the charade and crossed to her, wishing her sweater weren't pressed against her that way and glad that it was. "Knows what?"

"That we didn't fall into a snowdrift."

"I don't know about you," he said, tenderly pushing her hair behind her ear, "but I have the distinct impression that I fell into one. A very deep one."

All sorts of delicious things were happening to Eve as he touched her face. She felt herself melting, wanting to go with the definite flow of her liquefying bones.

"You'd better get into that shower," he instructed, his voice growing husky with longing. *Before I forget who and where we are and do something very, very stupid,* he added silently.

She saluted and walked off in front of him with what he could have sworn was a saunter.

Luke went into the bedroom and pulled out a clean pair of jeans and a shirt. He stripped off his own wet

clothing and let them fall in a sodden heap that he
kicked off to the side. With long, hard strokes he
rubbed a towel hard against his skin, intent on chaf-
ing it raw. The surge of friction he created did nothing to wipe the soft image of Eve from his mind. She
shimmered before him, warm, inviting.

"Forbidden fruit," he reminded himself, grabbing
his jeans. He found that his balance was dangerously
off as he dragged on one pant leg. He shifted quickly
to keep from falling. "Damned woman throws me off
balance no matter what I'm doing," he muttered to his
boots.

Dressed, he scooped up the dry things he'd laid out
and went to the bathroom door. He didn't hear any
water running. For a moment he toyed with the idea
of opening the door. The thought made him ache for
her again. If he kept this up, he told himself, he'd be
certifiably crazy by Christmas.

"I'll just lay these out here," he called to Eve.

The door opened just as he was bending over to de-
posit the neatly folded clothing on the floor in front of
it. He encountered a slim, nude leg. Systems within his
orderly mind began to go haywire. He looked up before he raised his head.

Wrapped in a towel, she embodied all the sweet,
pure things that had been part of his life once. How
the hell could anything look so sweet and so sexy at the
same time?

She could, he thought.

"You've changed," she remarked.

He picked up the clothes and handed them to her.
"Not so's you'd notice."

Always fighting her, she thought. "I mean your
clothes. Don't you want to take a shower, too?"

Yes, with you.

His eyes burned into her as he said, "Lady, all I want at this moment is to see how fast I can wrestle that towel away from you." He took a deep breath. "So if you know what's good for you, you'll get in that bathroom fast and lock the door."

Eve liked the way passion clouded his eyes, making them smoky.

"I'm not issuing any more warnings."

She retreated, not out of fear but with a soft compliance. "Yes, sir." She hugged the clothes against her breasts as she took a step backward. "And Luke?"

He pivoted on one heel, his shoulders tense. Just how much self-control did this woman think that he had? "Yeah?" he asked warily.

"I *do* know what's good for me." With her eyes she completed the statement: *you.*

Luke turned and walked to the door without another word. On his way out he picked up his spare jacket. It was suddenly way too hot for him inside the little cabin. And much too confining.

She had his number.

Or did she?

He had little time to ponder the problem. As soon as he got outside, he was surrounded by Alex, Kristin and Whiskey. For once, he was actually glad they were there.

Chapter Eight

Before he realized what was happening, Luke found himself surrounded by the children.

One and one definitely did not equal two, he thought. Not in this case. It equaled an army. A short one, but an army nonetheless. Kristin and Alex had abandoned the lopsided snowman they were making and completely overwhelmed Luke, looking up at him with supplicating eyes. Eyes that reminded him too much of Eve's. Whiskey bounded around him, tracing out a semicircle in the snow, barking at him and sending snow flying. Luke looked toward Chester expectantly, but no help was forthcoming from that quarter. He'd have to handle this group on his own.

"Well?" Luke looked from one small delicate face to the other. Alex turned shy suddenly and tugged on Kristin's sleeve, indicating that she should be the one to broach the subject.

Kristin in turn glanced over her shoulder to where Chester was resting his bulk against the woodpile.

"Don't look at me," he told her. "If you want something, you're going to have to speak up for yourself."

At least the old man didn't seem to take anyone's side, Luke thought absently, wondering whether he should be grateful. He looked back at the two up-turned faces. It annoyed Luke that the children appeared to be frightened of him. Well, what did he expect? His manner had been abrupt, right? And hadn't this been what he wanted? To keep them all at arm's length? So why did accomplishing that bother him so much?

Congratulations, Randall. You've sunk to a new low. Now you frighten children.

He tried to compose his face into an amiable expression.

Kristin looked down at her snow-covered mittens, then cleared her throat. She gazed up at Luke, determination in her eyes.

A lot like her mother, Luke thought, softening even more.

"It's Christmas Eve tomorrow," she said in a small, childish voice, then stopped.

"Yes?" His own voice sounded cold to his ear. Two sides warred within him. One fought for maintaining the status quo that was emerging; the other struggled to regain lost ground.

Kristin pressed on bravely. "There aren't any Christmas decorations in your cabin."

"No," Luke agreed, his voice patient, "there aren't."

"Are you Jewish?" Alex suddenly piped up. Kristin cuffed him into silence. Alex yelped and took a step backward, holding his ear.

"You don't ask people their religion, Alex," Chester interceded in a gruff voice. Alex glared at Kristin.

"No, I'm not Jewish," Luke answered for the sake of argument. What were they getting at?

"Then why aren't there any decorations?" Kristin was bewildered. "Don't you believe in Christmas?"

"It's not a matter of believing," Wasn't it? he asked himself. Wasn't it a matter of not believing in anything anymore, not even himself? Questions suddenly challenged him, questions that had lain dormant, frozen, like the scenery around him. Damn these people for coming into his life.

Kristin didn't seem to hear his protest. "Didn't you *ever* believe in Christmas?"

"Yes," Luke answered, remembering. His expression softened a little. "Once."

Alex stepped forward, grabbing on to Luke's sleeve, grabbing on to more than that. The boy seemed to be pleading with Luke. "Couldn't you believe in it again? Huh? Just for a little while?"

They made him uncomfortable, yet he couldn't just shake them, couldn't just walk away. Not anymore. "I don't know what my believing—"

Kristin took his hesitation as a sign of complete capitulation. She grabbed his hand excitedly. He was trapped between the two children. Even Whiskey seemed to be taking part in the siege, sitting down in the snow and raising the jumbled mess of fur that passed for a head in Luke's direction. If he looked beneath all that fur, Luke mused, there were probably soft, pleading eyes there, too. The entire family was bent on his undoing.

"There're lots of trees out here." Kristin gestured behind her with her free hand. "Couldn't we go get one?"

Was that what she was driving at? Chopping down a tree? A Christmas tree? For *his* cabin? "What?"

Kristin saw the incredulous look on Luke's face and swallowed hard, but Alex began to jump up and down. In his mind there was every chance in the world that Luke would agree. "Oh, please, Luke Randall. Please?"

No doubt about it; he was surrounded. He found that it wasn't an altogether unpleasant feeling. He looked over toward Chester. "Take after their mother, don't they?"

Chester gave away none of his thoughts as he studied Luke. "Yup."

"If we get this tree—" Luke began.

"Yay!" Alex cried, still jumping up and down and now yanking Luke's arm.

"If!" Luke repeated patiently. "We don't have anything to decorate it with."

Hope sprang into Kristin's face. "Oh, we'll find something," she assured him in a voice far more authoritative than her years would warrant.

"I'd say they got you outnumbered," Chester observed in his emotionless voice.

"Outnumbered for what?" Eve asked.

Luke turned and saw her standing in the doorway. She was wearing the clothes he'd left out for her and looked outrageously lost in them. Lost and utterly adorable. She'd rolled back the shirtsleeves so that they rested, thick and bulky, over her wrists. She'd done likewise with the cuffs of his jeans, which awk-wardly brushed the tops of her boots. A belt cinched the jeans at her waist, giving the effect of a denim wrapper pulled tight around a slender bouquet of wildflowers.

That was what she made him think of out here—spring and wildflowers, he realized.

The waistband on the jeans came almost up to her armpits, from what he could see. She'd folded one of the blankets and thrown it around her shoulders like a shawl. She looked like a lost waif—a lost waif who made his blood boil.

Eve saw his gaze travel up and down the length of her, saw the wide smile come to his lips. His whole face lit up when he smiled, she marveled. He looked to-tally different. Warm. Approachable. She wondered how she could get him to stay that way.

"You needn't laugh," she informed Luke with all the majesty of a princess. Her eyes gave her away, he thought.

A princess. What an odd idea. Funny how he could imagine her in almost any situation. And yet she seemed so unreal to him, so removed from all the ug-liness of the world.

Eve caught the strange expression on his face and knew he was sinking back into the mire of thought that had claimed him so completely less than three days ago. Say something! Don't lose him now.

"They're your clothes," she pointed out. She gave herself a D minus for content. Still, she saw the frown dissipate. Thank God, she thought. She upped her grade to a B plus.

"And never have they been filled out so, um, inter-estingly," he told her graciously.

Alex moved toward her, his head tilted, his expression stunned. "Mommy, you look like a circus clown."

She patted Alex on the head. "Thank you, darling. I can always count on you to boost my ego. So—" she raised her eyes to meet Luke's "—what is it they have you outnumbered for?"

"They want to—"

"Luke's going to get us a tree!" Kristin announced proudly, joining her mother. She turned her face toward Luke.

Eve put one arm around Kristin's shoulders and looked over her daughter's head at Luke, her brows raised daintily in surprise. "Oh?" There was no hiding the pleased look on her face.

He tried not to think about the fact that her smile of approval sent rays of warmth through him. "I didn't say—"

"Oh, please, Luke Randall, please?" Alex tugged his sleeve again.

"How do you manage with them?" Luke asked.

Eve grinned. "One day at a time, Luke. One day at a time." She pulled her arms closer, fending of the cold. "Now, about this tree you're getting—"

"I never said I—"

Eve ignored his words. "Can we wait until after lunch? My clothes'll be dry by then and I can come along to help."

"Us too!" Kristin chimed in.

"Don't I get a say in this matter?" Luke had already conceded the issue in his mind. All right, what would it hurt? They were children, and Christmas was for children, right? He was only doing it to keep them quiet, he reasoned. He refused to explore the matter any further.

"Of course you do," Eve told him lightly, touching his arm for emphasis.

It was as if two ends of an electrical wire had made contact. He saw her reaction in her eyes, even though she maintained an unchanged expression.

"As long as that say is yes," she finished.

"I—"

The ax he used to chop the firewood was leaning against the side of the house. Eve walked over to it and lightly placed her hand on the handle. "Of course, you don't have to come if you don't want to. You can just give me your ax and I'll—"

"Wind up cutting off your hand." He took it from her, shaking his head.

"If you say so," she said sweetly, turning around and walking back into the cabin. Luke watched her in silence for a moment as the children trooped in after her. Alex gave Luke a broad grin, then disappeared inside.

"She won, you know," Chester commented as he walked past Luke.

"Yeah, I know." The words weren't addressed to Chester. Luke realized he was talking to himself.

Sunshine nibbled at his soul.

Suddenly he had a great need to chop some more firewood. He had to do something in response to the adrenaline that was flooding through his body.

"I told you he was a good man," Eve called out to Chester when he entered the cabin.

He watched as she neatly refolded the blanket and put it back into the bedroom, and he followed her inside. "Yes, you told me."

His tone of voice made her frown. She stopped by the bed, studying him. "You don't have to sound as if that admission pains you."

"It doesn't." He put his large hands on her shoulders. "I'm just worried about you, Evie."

She might have known this was coming. He was still her mother and father all rolled up into one. "Me?"

He snorted, dropping his hands. "Don't give me that innocent look. You know perfectly well what I mean. You don't know anything about this man. Has he even told you what he's doing way up here all alone?"

She walked back into the living area. The children were playing with Whiskey by the fire. She gave them a smile as she walked by them.

"When's lunch, Mom?" Kristin asked.

"Soon." She glanced at Chester. "He's monitoring weather equipment."

Chester followed her as she made her way into the kitchenette. "Hmm. He acts more like a spy to me," he said suspiciously. He rubbed his chest thoughtfully.

Eve had begun rummaging through the pantry for something to serve for lunch. She peered up at her uncle. "A spy?" The idea was ridiculous. "What would he be spying on here? The bears?"

"No, but the equipment you said he had could be used to pick up—oh, I don't know—signals. Something." He continued to rub his chest as he talked.

Eve shook her head and went back to her search for food. Didn't the man have anything but stew? She shifted the cans around. She could just kill for a tuna salad with gobs of fresh mayonnaise and celery. "You're grasping at straws, Uncle Chester."

"Maybe." He eased his bulk into a chair. "But you're the only niece I have, Evie. You've had enough hurt in your life. No need to go looking for any more."

Oh, well, Eve conceded, another beef stew lunch wouldn't kill them. She pulled out two cans and set them on the counter. "I'm not looking," she told her uncle.

"But finding."

Eve took out the can opener from the drawer where Luke kept it. "Well, I can't ignore the man," she said evasively.

"No, but you don't have to go falling in love with him, either."

Startled, Eve opened her mouth.

"Go ahead—deny it." Chester waved his hand at her. "I won't believe you, anyway."

Eve regained her poise. Chester always could read her like a book. "I wasn't going to deny it."

"How can you fall in love with a man you've known for only three days!" he demanded, exasperated, and half rose in his seat. The children looked at him. He cleared his throat and sank back on the chair.

"I knew Shawn for only two before I was sure he was the right one," Eve reminded him gently. She opened the first can.

"That was pure luck," Chester said dismissively.

"Maybe," she conceded. A fierce, inexplicable urge to defend Luke came over her. "Besides, you were the one who said that I was in love with Luke," she reminded him. "I didn't."

He rubbed his chest hard. "You didn't deny it."

She grinned. "You said you wouldn't let me."

"Okay, I'll let you." He looked at her hopefully.

Eve dumped the contents of both cans into the battered metal pot. She kept her eyes on her work. "Sorry."

"Evie, you've got a heart as big as all outdoors, and you're incorrigible."

"I know."

He sighed. "I love you."

She looked up at Chester and winked. "Good."

After lunch, her arms loaded with her own clothes, Eve went into the bedroom to change while Chester washed the dishes. She was surprised that Luke grudgingly agreed to watch the children outdoors. Surprised and happy. The man was definitely coming around, she thought as she quickly slipped on her own clothes. They felt warm from the fire, and she felt warm from her own thoughts. All in all it wasn't a bad combination, she thought as she combed her hair.

As she walked out of the bedroom, Eve heard coming through the window the sound of childish voices raised in shouts of triumph.

"Sounds like Luke might need some help," she commented, smiling. She laid the neatly folded jeans and shirt on the coffee table and picked up her parka. It felt warm, almost delicious. She could have easily curled up in it. "I guess that's our cue to come to the rescue."

"Don't you always?" Chester mumbled, wiping his hands. He tossed the towel on the counter and walked around the side.

"Ready," she sang out as she opened the door and walked outside.

Luke dropped the snowball he'd been making. His eyes skimmed over Eve. Her jeans hugged her figure, and the sight of her generated a sudden longing within him. He banked down the feeling and grinned. "I think I preferred the other outfit."

Eve wasn't altogether sure how she should read that remark, but it sounded playful enough. "You would," she said, pretending to sniff. Alex and Kristin darted over to her side just as Chester came out of the cabin.

"Well, let's get this over with." Luke looked at the four people clustered near him. "But before we take two steps," he continued just as Alex walked into him. Luke steadied the boy with his hands and held him in place. "I don't want anyone wandering off. Is that clear?" His words were directed mainly toward Alex, but they took in everyone. The last thing Luke wanted was to have to search for one of them by himself.

It was a day out of a children's book, Luke thought as they trudged through the woods. Two kids, a dog, an old man, and a man and a woman. How had he let himself get roped into this? And why did something like this, so alien to his chosen way of life, feel so right?

He gripped his ax harder and walked on.

The children ran ahead with the dog darting around them. Luke had to call out a warning several times to keep them from running off. Behind him was Chester, bullishly determined to keep up, especially after Luke had suggested he stay behind in the cabin. Luke kept looking over his shoulder to make sure the old man was still there.

"He'll be all right," Eve whispered, walking alongside Luke.

"Who?"

"Uncle Chester. If you keep looking back, you're going to wound his pride."

"I'd rather have his pride wounded than have his body in some snowdrift."

She pushed back her hair, which the wind kept whipping into her face. She gave Luke a warm look. "Luke Randall, you are a thoroughly nice man."

Luke mumbled something under his breath, and Eve laughed.

"How about that one?" Alex cried excitedly, pointing at the thirty-foot tree directly behind him.

"We'd never fit it into the cabin," Luke replied dryly.

Alex gave it one last look. "Oh, couldn't we try?" he pleaded.

"Alex, don't be a dope," Kristin said haughtily. "We could only get a branch of that in." She looked all the way up at it, recalculating as she shaded her eyes. "Maybe not even. We want a whole tree, not just a piece."

"Whole trees are nicer, Alex," Luke explained, feeling compelled to soften Kristin's comment.

Alex brightened.

Luke caught Eve's eye. She was trying not to laugh. There was pure pleasure in her eyes. Why hadn't he met her ten years ago? And then these children would be his and—No, he couldn't let himself think like that. It could only lead to danger. The reality was that he *hadn't* met her ten years ago, and now was too late for both of them. He knew he could only hurt her. The Luke Randall of today had nothing to offer.

"This one, Luke."

He realized that Kristin was talking to him.

"What?"

"How about this one?" She stood in front of a tree that dwarfed her, though it was only about eight feet tall. "It's full and—" she stopped to inhale "—it *smells* so Christmasy." Suddenly she was as eager as her little brother. "Please?"

"Can't pass up a Christmasy-smelling tree," Luke said. He circled the tree and decided that it would do as well as any. He braced himself to take a swing when the dog ran out in front of him. Luke pulled his swing up short, his heart pounding. Had he swung any sooner, the ax would have connected with the animal. "Doesn't this dog of yours have any sense?" he yelled at Eve.

"None, I'm afraid," Eve admitted, grabbing hold of Whiskey's collar and pulling him out of the way.

He looked at Eve, mystified. "He can't find his way out of a paper bag. He must cost a fortune to feed, if the past couple of days are any indication. Why do you bother to keep him?"

Eve shrugged. He realized that the question had never even entered her mind and that she wasn't going to seriously consider it now. "I guess it's just like Uncle Chester says. I'm a sucker for a lost soul—and Whiskey was a lost, mangy dog when he turned up in our yard one morning."

Is that how she sees me? Luke wondered. A mangy, lost soul? He could tell by the whimsical look on her face that she was drawing some sort of analogy. "I didn't turn up in your yard—you turned up in mine."

She held her hands up innocently. "I never said a word."

"But you were thinking it," he growled.

"Now who's trying to read minds?"

Kristin interjected huffily, "Are you two going to talk all afternoon, or cut the tree?"

"Bossy," Luke muttered, curling his hands around the ax again.

"Sometimes," Eve conceded.

He glanced at Whiskey to make sure the dog was secured. "Like her mother."

"Maybe."

"No maybe about it." Luke took out his frustrations on the tree. It was down in short order.

"I'll take it back!" Alex bounded over before the tree had even hit the ground. He wrapped his hands around the sticky trunk. Making fierce faces of concentration, Alex tugged and tugged and the tree moved a fraction of an inch—backward.

Kristin put her hands on her hips. "Alex, let Luke do it."

"But I want to help!" Alex protested.

Luke looked at Eve, but she merely shook her head. She was throwing the ball in his court. On purpose. Luke could see that he wasn't going to have any peace unless he came up with some sort of compromise. "Pick up the tip," Luke told him.

Alex looked behind him at the very top of the tree. "That?" He pointed, crushed.

"That's where the star goes, isn't it?" Luke asked matter-of-factly.

Alex scratched his head. "Yes."

Luke kept his voice serious despite the fact that he caught Eve's nod of approval. This was *her* department, not his. But the annoyance he was trying to summon wouldn't come. "That's the most important part of the tree, wouldn't you say?"

A grin spread over Alex's face. "Yeah."

"Well, then, what are you waiting for? Go to it."

Alex scrambled through the snow to wind his fingers through the very top of the tree.

"You do that quite well," Eve told Luke sotto voce.

"What?" He looked at her, confused. "Cut a tree?"

"No," she answered simply, "join in a family."

"It's called survival instinct. I tend to adapt to whatever conditions I find myself in, no matter how taxing."

"Oh." Her expression told him that she wasn't buying any of it.

"Don't go making something out of this," he warned her.

"Me?"

"You. I just didn't want to hear him wailing and complaining for the rest of the day."

"I understand," she said placidly.

"Look—" he started again.

"Yes?" she asked, all innocence.

"Never mind." He clamped his mouth shut. There was just no arguing with the woman. She seemed convinced that she knew his motives better than he did.

And maybe she did, he realized. There was no denying the good feeling that had spread through him when he'd heard the children's squeals of joy. But the very act of gaining that reaction opened old wounds. Having them there, having her there, set him back two years. When they left, it was going to be a struggle for him to return to where he had been emotionally. A hell of a struggle.

When they left. The silent words had a hollow ring. He pushed them out of his mind. Holding on to the ax with one hand, he plunged the other between the lush branches until his fingers wrapped around the tree trunk. He began to lift it when he realized that Eve had joined in, on the other side.

"Isn't this too heavy for you?" he asked.

She shook her head. "I'm stronger than I look."

"I've already found that out," Luke muttered.

"Besides, you're holding up the bulk of the tree," she pointed out. She glanced over her shoulder. "You and Uncle Chester." She frowned slightly, and he immediately knew what she was thinking. This exertion, added to the trudge through the woods, might be too much for the old man.

"Actually," Luke said, stopping, "I'd have an easier time of it if there weren't so many helping hands tugging in all different directions. I just need one assistant. Alex?"

Alex's disappointed look turned to one huge smile. "Yes, sir!" He picked up the tip of the tree happily.

"This boy," Luke said to Eve as he picked up the trunk again, "can be trained."

Chester rubbed his chest absently in small circles. "He's not the only one," he said under his breath.

His words carried to Luke. He wondered just what the old man meant.

Chapter Nine

They brought the tree, snow and all, into the cabin. When Luke righted the wide-branched spruce and held it up for the children's inspection, it met with warm approval.

It took Luke nearly two hours to construct a stand that would hold the tree securely in place. He could have managed it, he felt, in less than an hour, but he had "help." Alex had insisted on being his first assistant and Kristin, never one to take a backseat to her little brother, provided another set of "helping" hands. Eve refereed, grateful that Luke had softened enough to indulge the children.

Luke drove the last nail into the stand, then stood up. His assistants were busy squabbling over something. "Is it my imagination, or are they getting louder?"

He watched as Eve slowly brushed pine needles from the front of his shirt. Her fingertips gliding across his chest seemed to sear right through the material.

"They're getting used to you," she explained.

"Terrific." He pretended to be preoccupied with the children. But he suspected that Eve saw right through him. He waved his hammer toward them. "I take it, then, that this is what they're normally like."

She took the hammer from him and put it on the desk. "More or less," she said almost absently, toying with one of the buttons on his shirt. It was half out of the hole and she pushed it back through. She wasn't being coy, just trying to make herself keep her hands off him. This wasn't the time or the place to do the things that were filling her head right now, she knew.

Luke realized that she was physically and emotionally disarming him. He clung to the conversation. "Lady, I don't envy you." Her nearness, the look in her eyes, seemed to speak to him. He felt she was telling him that she was experiencing the same things he was right now. He tried to dismiss it all as just his imagination. How could a simple look say so much?

Eve dropped her hand to her side, looking at her children. "Oh, it's not so bad." She turned her attention back to him. "Besides, I've noticed you seem to fare pretty well with them."

"That's the survival instinct I was telling you about," he reminded her. "Okay," he addressed his two less-than-able assistants, "let's see if she flies."

Alex's brows twisted together. "Trees don't fly," he cried, puzzled.

"It's just an expression, Alex," Kristin informed him condescendingly.

Luke tried not to smile. "Chester—" he looked over toward the seated man "—do you want to be part of this?"

Chester shuffled forward. "I *am* part of this."

"Don't I know it," Luke said under his breath. What had possessed him to try to make a gesture? Those damn blue eyes of hers, that's what. "Grab a section." He nodded toward the tree.

Together he and Chester righted the tree in the middle of the living area, where it tottered for a moment. Its branches shivered and swayed, dropping a few more needles on the wooden floor. Finally, it seemed to settle down.

"Well?" Luke said. Why he even cared what they thought of his handiwork was beyond him.

Kristin looked at the tree for a long, serious moment. "It's the most beautiful tree I've ever seen," she declared solemnly.

Eve put her arms around Kristin's shoulders. "That says it for me." She was looking at Luke, not the tree. Everything about her manner said "thank you" to him.

A warm feeling spread through Luke as he glanced away. It was getting harder and harder for him to maintain even a shred of the barrier he'd put up around himself, the one that kept him from hurting someone again. He met Alex's thoughtful gaze.

"It needs decorations," Alex pronounced.

Luke frowned.

"But it's a very pretty tree," the boy added hastily, afraid of offending.

Eve laughed and tousled Alex's hair. "I'm afraid that we're going to have to use our imaginations this year, darling. Mr. Randall's probably fresh out of decorations.''

Alex twisted around to look up at her. ''Can't we put somethin' on it 'sides our imaginations, Mom?''

She hated dampening his spirits, but there was nothing she could do. ''I don't—'' Eve began.

''He's got computer paper!'' Kristin cried suddenly. ''On the closet floor. I saw it.''

Eve looked at her daughter. ''Kristin, you're not supposed to go prowling through Mr. Randall's belongings.''

''Why not?'' Luke cut in, looking pointedly at Eve. ''Her mother goes prowling through my mind.''

''Okay.'' Eve folded her arms in front of her chest. ''What are you doing with computer paper?''

''They've been threatening to send up a computer here for a couple of months. First they gave me the supplies.'' He turned away. Even now, probably without her knowledge, her eyes were doing things to him, making him want her. Luke looked down at Kristin. ''What is it you want to do with the computer paper?''

Kristin was off and running. Not unlike her mother, Luke couldn't help thinking. She hooked his arm with hers and pulled him toward the bedroom, specially toward the closet and the cache of computer paper. ''All sorts of things. I can make stars, lanterns, angels—and we can use the sides for a chain.''

''Sides?'' he repeated, confused.

''You know, the part you pull off after the paper is ready.'' Alex, not to be outdone or forgotten, took hold of Luke's other arm and was manfully tugging him in the same direction.

Eve looked very dubious. There was such a thing as
going too far, and she was afraid that in their enthu-
siasm about Christmas, the children might have just
managed to plunge over that line. "Kristin," she
called after her daughter, walking into the bedroom
behind them, "I really don't think that Mr. Randall..."

But Luke had already disappeared into the closet
and retrieved the large box of paper. He passed Eve
and carried it back into the living area, where he deposited it on the floor next to the barren tree.

"Go ahead—let them," he said. "It would serve
Bruce right."

"Bruce?" Was Bruce someone else out of Luke's
secret past? She hoped that perhaps another gap had
formed in his protective armor.

Luke wondered why she wanted to know about
Bruce. He turned to face her. "My boss at the weather
station."

"Oh." So much for taking another leap forward,
she thought.

He stepped out of the way as Kristin and Alex
pounced on the bounty he placed at their feet. He
asked Eve, "What's the matter? You look disappointed."

"It's nothing." She kept her eyes on Alex as he
dived into the box for his share of paper. It followed
him out like a white accordion. "I just thought that
perhaps Bruce was someone out of your past."

So that was it. No, Eve, you can't come in any further. But he kept his voice gentle. "My past stays that
way, Eve. Don't mess with it."

"Someone has to," she insisted, keeping her voice
down. The children didn't appear to be listening, but

you never knew with children. She walked over to the sofa, out of the way.

He felt a frustrated anger come over him as he followed her. "Why?" he asked. She turned her face up to his. An old cliché, iron butterfly, flashed across his mind.

"Because you're not happy the way you are," she replied simply.

There she went again. "Lady, no one told you you could come in and try to rearrange my life. I'm happy with things just the way they are." But he wasn't and he knew it. He hadn't been happy, hadn't been anything. Just merely existing, day to day, no thoughts, no pleasures, no emotions. After the traumatic awakening he'd gone through in that back alley in Philadelphia, he had felt rage, pain, shock. His survival instinct had taken over to protect him, severing him from everything until he could come to terms with it.

And now she came into his life, she and her sunshine, her hope, making him remember what it was like to feel. She brought back memories of what his life had once been, of what he had once been. Of a life he had lost. And she was interfering with his healing process.

Eve held up a finger, disputing his words. "You're happy now," she declared, "in the thick of things."

"No," he insisted. Damn, why did she have to have such a tempting mouth? "But I was happy before."

"When before?" Eve challenged, raising on her toes. Her voice went up as she did. "Before we walked in, or before you came up here in the first place?"

It was the first time he had ever heard her raise her voice. The children stopped what they were doing, although Chester went right on laying out paper. Whisky began to bark and broke the tension.

"You're confusing me, Eve." It was an honest answer. He no longer knew what to believe.

She blew out a sigh and her good humor was instantly restored. "Good. It's a start. Now, do you have any scissors, pencils, tape?"

He laughed. "Don't ask for much, do you?"

"No more than you can deliver, Luke." Her smile was enigmatic.

In the next hour, his cabin floor, he thought, was transformed into a scene out of a Walt Disney movie. A perfectly matched girl and boy lay sprawled out on the wooden floor, doing their best to produce works of art. A giant mongrel kibitzed between them. And a gnomelike old man was sitting in a rocker by the fireplace, content to just watch and offer a word or two of advice from time to time. He rubbed his chest in rhythm to his rocking.

And how are you supposed to fit into all this? Luke asked himself as he pulled the perforated edges off the paper.

Nowhere.

The chain he was working on snapped in half. Alex looked up at him from his vantage place on the floor. "Not very good at this, are you?"

"Nope."

"How come?"

Why were they always plying him with questions? "I've never done this before. Hand me that stapler, Alex." Alex scrambled to obey. Luke stapled the ends together.

Alex patted his shoulder. "You'll get better with practice."

"This is all the practice I intend to get," Luke replied as he twisted off the next layer.

Eve, busy making paper birds at the table, surveyed the scene and felt a glow of contentment. She rose and approached Luke. Could he tell how she felt? she wondered. She squatted down, resting her hand on his shoulder for balance.

He looked up from what he was doing, sensing she wanted to tell him something. A long, delicate chain of white, perforated spaghetti coiled itself in his lap. "What?"

"You look happy."

"Eve," he rose and the chain dropped to the floor, "don't make assumptions."

"Aw, Mom," Kristin cried, "now look what you've done. He stopped working."

Luke picked up the remaining pile of paper. "Here." He handed his job over to Chester. "Take over for me."

"Quitting?" Chester asked.

Luke realized the question was loaded. He regarded the old man, then tempered his reply. "'Retiring' has a better ring to it."

Chester shrugged, turning his attention to the paper. He pulled at one edge. "Same difference."

Luke opened his mouth to retort, but Eve pulled him aside. "Luke, please," she whispered.

He kept his voice down for her sake, but the exasperation was impossible to miss. "You know, you people really do think you seem to have cornered the market on the right way to live."

She understood his irritation and tried to soothe it. "I'm sorry. When someone has something precious, it's only natural to share."

He felt his anger ebbing. "You know, you have a way of disarming an argument."

"That's *my* survival instinct," she told him.

He shook his head, then began to walk away.

"Where are you going?" she asked.

"To the loft."

"To get away?"

Yes, his mind shouted, but she looked so distressed he couldn't voice his thought. "No, I thought I saw something up there that you might use for the top of the tree."

With a self-satisfied smile, Eve let out a sigh of relief.

"If you keep looking so smug about it, I might change my mind," he warned with a grin. He watched as she made an elaborate motion of wiping the smile off her face. Whatever she did, he thought, she couldn't wipe it away from her eyes.

And it was her eyes that held him captive, whether he was willing to admit it or not. He turned his back on her and climbed up into the loft. He needed breathing space, he told himself.

Constrained into a crouching position, he began to search through the boxes in the attic. Luke had bought the cabin from an old man who had lived there forty years. Suddenly wanting to make use of his final remaining years, the man had gladly accepted Luke's offer. He'd taken only the clothes on his back when he had left. The boxes in the attic bore silent testimony to forty forgotten years of living.

The light was poor, to say the least. Luke turned around to go fetch a flashlight. When he heard footsteps on the ladder, he expected to see Alex, but Eve's head appeared in the opening.

"Hi," she said brightly, holding her hand out to him. After a beat he took it and helped her into the room. "It sure is dusty up here." She stood up and slapped a little off her jeans.

He sat back on his heels and eyed her suspiciously. "What are you doing up here?"

She looked down at him. "Oh, don't worry. I didn't come up to invade your inner sanctum."

"You've already done that," he pointed out.

"I'm here to help you look." She squinted around the dark corners of the cluttered room. Were all those boxes his? "Everyone knows men can't find anything."

"This, from a woman who lost an entire band of hikers?"

He watched as she shrugged, unaffected by his comment. He wished he were as unaffected by every movement of her slender, inviting body.

"Everyone's entitled to one mistake," she said.

And you're mine, Luke thought.

She drew closer to him. Hold me, Luke. I want you to admit that you need me as much as I need you.

Luke couldn't read her expression in the darkness, but he sensed it, felt it in every pore. He reached out and touched her face.

"I thought I saw a Christmas angel up here," he told her slowly, his mind light-years away from his topic. She was filling his mind, leaving room for nothing else. "A real one," he amended, remembering that he had referred to her that way. "The old guy I bought the cabin from was a traditional sort. I thought that maybe..." The hell with the angel. "No chance of our sending the kids to the movies, is there?'' he asked wryly. "Something like *Lassie Come Home*, so that even Whiskey would be captivated.''

She shook her head slowly, her eyes on his face. "It's your own fault, you know, for not having a television set,'' she chided him. "A good movie would keep them all occupied for hours. Uncle Chester loves old movies. The older the better.''

He cupped her face with his hands. "That's because he was probably around when they were invented.''

She laughed. Silver chimes in the autumn wind, he thought. Her eyes fluttered shut as his fingertips lightly grazed her face. He continued. "But he'd probably be up here every few minutes, checking on us as if we were some pubescent couple necking in the back seat of an old car.''

I want to make love to you, Eve.

"That sounds good to me,'' she murmured a little breathlessly.

Startled, he realized she couldn't possibly be talking about what he was thinking. "What does?'' Gently, he swept away a strand of hair from her face.

"Necking. Kiss me, Luke. I don't want to have to make the first move every time, but my self-control vanishes around you.''

"That makes two of us,'' he whispered against her ear.

Eve shivered at his words. She felt the familiar pull in her lower abdomen, the yearning. They were both on their knees now, and despite her feelings, she couldn't help wondering out loud.

"Luke?''

"Hmm?''

"Why are you on your knees here?''

He laughed at her serious tone. "Haven't you noticed?" Slowly he traced the outline of her face with his fingertips. "The ceiling accommodates only short people and sugar plum fairies."

"And what am I?" she breathed. Touch me, Luke. Love me.

"My downfall, Eve. My salvation. Everything." He leaned back suddenly and pulled her to him, knocking the air out of her lungs. His words were true, he realized. He honestly didn't know whether loving her would be good or bad at this point. She brought him in contact with the past, and he didn't know whether he should face that or close it off forever. All he knew was that he wanted her.

Carefully, he fitted her body against his. Excitement pulsed through Eve. She could feel his growing desire and it brought a happiness to her like none she had ever experienced.

Luke cupped her face again, burying his fingers in her silver-blond hair. Watching her eyes, he drew her mouth to his, her warm, sweet breath on his face thrilling him to no end.

He must care, she thought. He would let go of his control only for something that meant a lot to him. She clung to that as she kissed him over and over again.

"Eve, if you're not careful, you might wind up with more than you can handle," he warned her in a husky voice.

He saw how her eyes shone, and he groaned. He had found and lost his soul again, lost it in her eyes this time. He felt free. Whatever logic had held his mind firmly entrenched before was gone now. He couldn't reason, couldn't do anything but feel and react.

He moved, and she shifted until she was beneath him. Her hair spilled out on the dusty floor like a ray of sunshine that had found its way through the cracks.

He ran the back of his hand along her cheek. "You're getting dirty."

"It'll wash away."

He smiled ruefully, aching—and wishing he weren't. "I'm either getting you wet or dirty or—"

Her expression told him she understood that he was trying to hide behind banter again. "Don't be afraid of feeling, Luke," she whispered. "It's only me."

She saw through him at every turn, he thought. But he was glad of it, glad to have someone to take this awful burden from him and make him not care about it or anything else.

He wanted to lose himself in her. Forever. He had no idea what salvation was like, but if it existed, it stood no more than five-foot-two and had silver-blond hair and the kindest eyes ever created.

He felt he wasn't capable of love anymore. But if he were capable, if that gift were still available to him, he thought, then he would have been in love with her.

The idea of loving her washed over him, bathing him in its luminous light. It had a healing power all its own.

He took his fingers from her face and slid them under her sweater, reverently touching her silken skin as if this were the first time he had ever touched a woman, the first time he had ever touched her. And in an odd way it was, he realized.

He heard her catch her breath as she moved beneath his hands. He paused. If she stopped him now, he didn't know whether he could survive the pain. But better now than later.

She took his hesitation for uncertainty. "Luke?" She whispered. "It's all right." She guided his hands back to her.

He pulled her sweater away from her skin, trying to bridle his impatience. He pressed his face against her lace covered breasts, placing a blanket of kisses on her warm skin.

Eve felt him undo the front clasp on her bra, freeing her for him as she slid deeper and deeper into a solid envelope of heat. She moved her hands up under his shirt, nimbly touching, possessing, reveling in the sensation of his skin against hers. Her heart hammered in her throat as he pressed his chest against hers, his tongue lightly grazing the throbbing pulse in her throat. She pulled him tighter against her.

She felt tears gathering in her eyes. He wanted her. He *needed* her. She needed to make a difference in someone's life. She now knew that she made a difference in his.

Chapter Ten

Momma! Momma, come quick!"

Kristin's screams jolted Luke and Eve into awareness of the world outside their own sphere. His body tensed as Eve sat bolt upright.

"Momma!"

Panic washed over Eve. She quickly refastened her bra and yanked her sweater down, looking at Luke with frightened eyes. "She never calls me Momma anymore."

Luke needed no further prompting. Pushing his shirttail hurriedly back into the waistband of his jeans, he preceded Eve down the ladder in quick, sure movements. Expecting anything, he still wasn't prepared for what he ultimately saw.

"What the...?"

Eve bumped into his solid back as she tumbled down the steps a fraction of a second behind him. Moving around the barrier of his body, she saw what it was that had made Kristin scream for her and had frozen Luke in his tracks. Her hand flew to her mouth as the panic within her mushroomed, overcoming her. Chester was lying facedown on the floor.

Frightened by Kristin's reaction, Alex clutched at his mother's other hand. "Momma, he just fell over." Alex looked at her uncertainly, his face holding a mute appeal. "I thought he was playing a game."

Eve forced her mind to respond. She looked toward Luke, a plea for help in her eyes. But he had already dropped to his knees beside the old man. As he simultaneously loosened clothing and searched for a pulse, Luke's agitated movements belied the calm on his face. She wanted to help, to do something—*anything*. But she knew she'd only be in the way. It took considerable willpower to remain where she was.

She dropped her hand from her mouth. "No," she heard herself saying hollowly. "It's not a game, honey. Uncle Chester is very, very sick." She pressed her lips together, keeping the cry out of her voice. "Luke?"

She wanted him to tell her that her uncle was really all right, that it was something minor, just a fainting spell. She wanted the same comfort that Alex was asking for. She felt frightened and ashamed at the same time.

Kristin threaded her icy fingers through her mother's other hand, gripping it tightly. Eve squeezed back, her eyes never leaving Luke.

Luke searched for the carotid artery, pressing three fingers on Chester's neck slightly below the base of his jaw. He felt it barely beating. "There's a pulse," he told Eve. "It's faint, but it's there." He watched Chester's stout chest. "He's not breathing, Eve." Luke barely glanced in her direction. There was no time to offer any comforting words. He had to concentrate all his energy on Chester. "I think he's having a heart attack."

"Oh, God." Eve stifled a sob. She couldn't give way, not now, not in front of the children.

But they were snowed in, she thought desperately. There was no way to get help.

He was going to die.

The thought throbbed in her temples. Even if help came, it might be too late. No! Everything in her rebelled against defeat. Something had to be done. Luke would find a way. He *had* to. She put her faith entirely in Luke.

"Luke—" she began.

He didn't hear her. He was trying to remember what he had been taught in the last first aid class he had taken.

Think, dammit, think! he ordered himself.

Suddenly it all came back to him. In his mind's eye he saw it as clearly as if there were a demonstration actually in progress. Making sure there was nothing blocking Chester's airway, he tilted the old man's head back and gave him mouth-to-mouth breathing. Adrenaline began to pump through Luke as his movements grew more sure. He watched the old man's chest for signs of movement. None. Telling himself not to panic, Luke went through the process again. And again.

A huge wave of relief washed over Eve. She realized what Luke was doing. Still squeezing Kristin's hand, Eve closed her eyes and offered up a fervent prayer.

Don't let him die like this. Please, not so close to Christmas. The children would never be the same.

They need him. We all need him. He's not so old, not really. Please, dear God, please...

The effort to contain her tears nearly drained her. She opened her eyes. Luke was still working on Chester. There was no change. She felt stinging tears form at the corners of her eyes. Kristin was squeezing her hand so hard that her fingers were almost numb.

The young girl stood watching, scarcely breathing. "Is Uncle Chester going to die, Momma?" she asked in a small voice.

"No, darling, he's not."

The fierceness in her voice broke through the haze around Luke. He wished he had her conviction. Without stopping to even look up in her direction, he repeated the whole procedure, his actions growing more and more urgent. It *had* to work.

"Live, damn you. Live!" he ordered the supine figure on the floor. Sweat was pouring into Luke's eyes. He blinked it away. "Don't you give up on me now, old man! Do you hear me?"

"Why's he yelling at Uncle Chester like that?" Alex cried, now thoroughly frightened.

"Hush, sweetheart, hush," Eve said in a voice that would brook no further questions. Her gaze never left Luke.

"Who's an old man?" The question was faint, the words slurred and whispered, but they were there.

Luke sank back on his heels, sucking in air. He suddenly realized that he'd forgotten to breathe. He passed his arm over his forehead, mopping up the sweat. "You are, and you're going to get older." Luke grinned at him broadly.

"Damned right I am," Chester rasped, too weak to move. His eyelids fluttered for a moment, and thinking the old man was going to pass out again, Luke remained poised, ready to do whatever was necessary to keep the man alive.

Chester's eyes fluttered open again. "You're going to have to help me up, boy."

Eve didn't remember dropping Kristin's hand or even how she got to Chester's side. "Stroke?" she asked.

Luke shook his head. "Too soon to tell. Could be just a reaction to the heart attack. He's not out of the woods yet. Not by a long shot."

"And damned well might never be...if you don't raise anyone on...that radio of yours," Chester managed to mumble.

"If he did have a heart attack, it certainly didn't do anything to sweeten his disposition," Luke observed, relieved to hear the man talking. A fighting spirit could mean all the difference in the world.

"Didn't have to. Sweet enough already." Chester's eyes closed.

Eve pulled in her breath. "Luke?"

Luke checked his vital signs. They were there. He rocked back on his heels. "He's just asleep, Eve."

"He can't stay here on the floor," Kristin insisted. "It's not comfortable."

"I don't think he cares very much about how comfortable he is," Eve answered, still looking at the very pale face that she loved so well. He would live. And Luke had performed a miracle.

She looked at him with new wonder. Who *was* this man?

If he felt her eyes on him, he gave no indication.

"Maybe not, but she has a point," Luke agreed, rising. He gazed at the bulky form for a long moment. It wasn't going to be easy. "I'm going to see if I can get him onto the bed."

Chester was shorter, but he easily had fifty pounds on Luke. Eve looked from her uncle to Luke. "Do you think you should?"

"I've had training in this sort of thing," he assured her. He squatted. "I know what I'm doing."

She moved to help him. "I never said you didn't."

He gave her a quick, intimate look, then turned very businesslike. In clipped sentences he told her exactly where to place her hands, what to do and what not to do. Between the two of them, with Alex holding on to Whiskey to keep the dog out of the way, they managed to get Chester into the bedroom. Kristin hastily pulled back the blankets just as they deposited great-uncle's bulky form on the bed.

Eve's sweater was soaked with perspiration from the effort, and she felt shaken down to the very bottom of her foundation. She didn't trust her legs to support her. She pushed her hair out of her face as she adjusted the blanket around her sleeping uncle, then turned to look at Alex. "I want you and Kristin to stay here with Uncle Chester while I get some coffee. Call me if anything changes. Anything at all—understand?"

The children, greatly subdued, nodded solemnly and accepted her trust. They sat cross-legged on the floor, their eyes never leaving their great-uncle's slumbering form.

"Will he be all right, Mother?" Kristin asked just before Eve left the room.

Eve paused, her hand on the door. "He's going to be just fine."

She followed Luke out. "Am I lying?"

"I don't know. I'm not a doctor," he told her honestly, crossing to the shortwave radio. In all the excitement of the late afternoon, he'd forgotten to try to see if he could establish contact with anyone. Now the act took on that much more importance.

Eve stood by the desk, looking at him, her mind crowded with a thousand emotions and sensations. "Just what *are* you, Luke Randall?"

He looked at her for a long, silent moment. "Does it matter?"

"Yes. It does. To me. It matters that you trust me enough to tell me."

He didn't answer immediately. Instead he tried to raise someone on the shortwave. But it gave less of a response than it had that morning. There wasn't even a squawk. "Damn. There *has* to be somebody there."

"What happens if you can't get anyone?"

He leaned back in his chair and gave her a long, studious look. "You sound awfully bleak, for someone so full of sunshine."

She put her hand over his. "Luke," she said, "what happens?"

"I don't know. Maybe this was just a mild attack. Maybe he'll be all right on his own." He raked his hand through his hair. It had been some evening, he thought. He felt three steps past exhausted. "But I, for one, would feel a whole lot better if we could get him to a hospital."

She sat down on the desk top. "So would I.... Luke," she began.

He looked up at her. "Yes?"

"I haven't thanked you."

He saw the expression on her face, the relief that was etched there, the love in her eyes. Briefly he touched her cheek, then withdrew his hand. "Yes you have," he told her softly.

He took her hand for a moment and she was content just to let him hold it, to let him feed her great need for comfort. But presently her mind came back to the question he'd left unanswered. "Luke, where did you learn how to do that?"

"Holding hands comes naturally to a man."

"Luke, I'm serious." She looked into his face and saw a wall of pain forming in his eyes. He was remembering something, she thought. What had just happened had triggered some memory that had to be released, something he had buried. She pushed aside her own grief, her own need to be held, to be comforted. He needed her more. She had to break through to him—now, while the new barrier was still weak. "Talk to me, Luke, really talk to me. Who are you, and why are you here? What drove you away? I want to hear."

"No you don't."

"Try me."

He let go of her hands and leaned back in the chair, studying her, his face hard, impassive. There were no clues for her there. She had no idea whether she was winning or losing this battle. Finally he nodded. "All right, I'll tell you."

She felt anticipation and fear mingle. She said nothing. Her palms felt damp against the desk top.

"I was a policeman in Philadelphia." A bitter smile curved his lips. "It was something I always wanted to be. I had plans, dreams that I could make a difference, at least in my own neighborhood." How could anyone ever have been so naive? he thought.

"It wasn't the kind of neighborhood where you could walk home safely at night. Not alone. It had been when I was a kid, but that was before the pushers, the dealers, moved in and changed everything." He closed his eyes, remembering. Eve saw the bitterness in his face.

"The good families that could afford to go moved out. The ones who couldn't sank in the mire. It was a standing joke that you had to shoot your way out of my neighborhood—with either a gun or a syringe. My brother Brian picked the latter."

"Oh, Luke." She touched his shoulder, trying to reach him, trying to give him some measure of comfort. But he was too far away; he was back in Philadelphia.

"I was the one who found him in his room. There was nothing I could do. It was too late." His voice was stony. But he couldn't keep back the pain. That would always stay fresh. "It was going on right under my roof and I didn't even know it. I was too busy trying to save everyone else." His voice was raw, angry.

"He lived with you?"

Luke nodded. "They both did—he and Teresa. My folks are dead."

She and Luke had that in common, Eve thought, feeling even closer to him.

"I didn't even know," he repeated incredulously. He ran his hand through his hair again, clearly shaken as he relived the memory. "Teresa knew, but she was too afraid to tell me, too afraid that it would split up the family. It did anyway," he said with irony. "After Brian died, I found out who his contact was. I wanted to kill the bastard with my bare hands." He looked at

Eve, his dark eyes flat, fathomless. "I would have, there and then, if I'd gotten my hands on him."

He paused, and Eve held her breath, waiting, knowing she had pushed him as far as she could. The rest of it was up to him. He had to tell her on his own, if they were to build any sort of relationship. "I got my chance during a stakeout the next week."

An icy wind passed over her. "You killed him?"

He looked at her, his expression sardonic. "Would that surprise you?"

She nodded slowly. "I can't see you killing anyone in cold blood."

He reached out and wound a silver curl around his finger. It was something to divert his mind. "See? You don't know me at all, Christmas angel. I thought about it a thousand times before that confrontation in the alley."

But it didn't make any sense, Eve thought. There was something wrong with what he was telling her. She didn't believe it. "*Did* you kill him?"

He shrugged. "I got him in the knee and the shoulder."

Relief washed over her, for the second time that evening. "Then you didn't kill him."

"No." He let go of the strand of her hair and sat up. "Eve, don't you understand? I *wanted* to kill him. That's the point. I wanted to kill him," he enunciated slowly, painfully. "I became as bad as the people I was putting behind bars. I came face-to-face with myself in that alleyway, and I didn't like what I saw, what I had become."

He blew out a breath harshly. "I didn't make a difference in their world. I didn't free the neighborhood of scum. I became precisely what I was sworn to hunt down. I had to get away from there before I could be corrupted any further, before *I* corrupted anyone any further. So I moved Teresa out, got her settled in a better part of town, saw that she was provided for, and I came out here, where I wouldn't contaminate anything. And where nothing could touch me.''

Eve rose to her feet. Suddenly, she was holding on to him, her arms around him like a shield. "Oh, Luke, Luke, you're not corrupt."

He pulled back from her, turning away. "You're not thinking clearly. I just saved your uncle's life. You don't know what you're talking about.''

But she wouldn't let him get away. She jerked on his arm until he swung around. "Dammit, I do. You're not evil, just human. You can't go on punishing yourself for your brother's death or because you weren't Superman. And burying yourself here for so long is a waste. You can't keep on shutting yourself out of your own life!''

"What the hell are you talking about?''

"You're cheating yourself," she insisted, not relenting. "The Luke Randall who existed, who bled when he saw the raw side of life—he's still there." She tapped his chest. He drew back as if she had burned him. She wanted to scream at him, make him understand. He made her feel totally frustrated, at a loss for words to make him see.

"You've just dammed him up. That drug dealer didn't just kill your brother—he almost succeeded in killing you, too. Come back, Luke," she pleaded. "Come back and face the man you really are. You were idealistic—"

"I was stupid," he spat out.

All right, she'd concede that if she could get him to come around, she thought. "That, too, maybe."

Her glib acknowledgment stopped him for a second. He realized he was vaguely amused by her choice of verbal defense. "Are you looking for a fight?"

She sighed. She had a feeling that maybe the worst was over. At least the black look on his face was gone. "I'm looking to avoid one."

She had a damned funny way of going about it, he thought.

A small smile formed on her lips. "You're not running from me anymore, Luke. I won't let you." She placed her hands on his neck, lacing her fingers together. "Besides, everything happens for a reason. Maybe it all had to happen this way so that you would be here to save us."

He stared at her, awestruck by the hopelessly optimistic way she saw everything.

"Did you ever stop to think that maybe things *didn't* have to happen the way they did? If you hadn't gotten lost on the mountain, then my being here wouldn't have mattered."

He couldn't shake her, he saw. "You're just trying to complicate a simple belief," she replied.

"The belief might be incredibly simple, but there's certainly nothing simple about you."

Luke took her into his arms. For the moment, he surrendered. Despite the fact that he felt drained from telling her his secret, from fighting death for the soul of that old man who meant so much to her, he felt a flare of desire coursing through him. Above all else, he still wanted her. It had nothing to do with the fact that he hadn't had a woman in his arms, in his bed, in two years. There was something about her that stirred him. His isolation only intensified his reaction to her. He would have wanted her if he had run into her at the social club he used to frequent on the South side.

Picturing her there, amid people he'd known all his life, made him smile.

She traced the smile lightly with the tip of her finger. "What is it?"

He kissed her finger. "Nothing."

"Tell me, Luke."

He put the image aside. "You've turned me completely inside out in three days."

She tilted her head and kissed him softly on the lips. "I must be slipping. It should have only taken two."

He sat back down and pulled her onto his lap, then pressed a kiss to her temple. Gently he rocked her, enjoying her warmth. "Eve, Eve, this is all wrong."

"No," she told him firmly, brushing her lips quickly against his. "This is all right." She put her arms around his neck again. "And the sooner you start believing that, the better you'll feel."

She wanted to stay there, on his lap, forever. But there were things to see to, other people to think of. She blew her bangs away from her forehead. "I'd better look in on Chester and the children."

She began to rise. Reluctantly he let her go, then stood up next to her. "I've never had to use my first aid training before. I've never saved a man's life before."

She grinned up at him. "See? Doing good deeds all the time. You're not the monster you keep telling yourself you are."

Despite her light tone, Eve held her breath as she walked back into the bedroom. She found Kristin and Alex lying on the floor, asleep, the whole ordeal having proved too much for them. Apprehensively Eve moved over toward the bed to watch her uncle. Chester was still sleeping peacefully. She knew the sound of his breathing well enough to feel heartened at the steady rhythm.

She didn't have to turn around to know exactly when Luke entered the room. All her senses seemed to come alive at once.

She gestured at her uncle. "Consider that your first miracle," she whispered to Luke.

The first miracle in my life, Luke nearly said aloud, was you. But habits were hard to break. He kept his silence.

She looked back at her children. "I'd better get them into their sleeping bag." She pushed up the sleeves on her sweater.

"Need help?"

She took no pains to hide her grateful smile. "I'd love it."

Fifteen minutes later, she was in the kitchen, making coffee. She felt as if she could drink a gallon. Luke was back at his desk, working the dials of the radio, still talking into the stillness and getting no reply. She brought over a mug for him and one for herself, then dragged over the rocker that Chester had favored. She sat down on the edge, her knees pressed together.

He snapped off the radio. He'd try again later.

They talked about everything and anything, and as the night wore on, Luke felt as if he was working his spirit free. There was something so pure about Eve, so hopeful, that for a moment he tapped into it himself.

Maybe things could work out for him, he thought. For them. Maybe she was right. Maybe he wasn't the tainted creature he thought he had become.

Chapter Eleven

Eve felt herself being lifted slowly. Something strong and powerful was holding her, making sure she wouldn't fall. Strong and powerful, yet gentle. She sighed and relaxed. She felt safe and protected.

Luke looked down at the sleeping woman in his arms. Eve curled her face into his chest. She had fallen asleep in the chair, waiting for him to reach someone on the shortwave radio. Luke thought he had never held anything so precious before. Careful not to wake her, he carried her to the sofa and gently set her down. She murmured something in her sleep. He bent to catch what she was saying, but the words were gone.

Just as she would be in a day or two. Or sooner. He straightened, wondering why he was doing this to himself, why he was letting himself become enmeshed when he knew that ultimately nothing could come of it.

Nothing but pain.

Luke sighed as he covered Eve with a blanket, then lightly tucked it around her. The temperature outside was dropping again, and it was beginning to get cold in the cabin. He turned and poked the fire, putting in another piece of wood. The fire snapped and crackled greedily, with renewed vigor. He stared into the hypnotic blaze, yet saw nothing.

He had to stop acting this way, he told himself, had to stop feeling this way. There was no future in loving her. He had to face reality. And reality was that her life was out there somewhere, with her children and the old man. Caught up in the thick of things. And his was nowhere any longer, he realized. It had been here in the wilderness up until a few days ago, but now...

Luke turned and looked at Eve's face as she slept. Her lower lip pouted a little, and she looked like a child. An innocent child who had touched his life.

What if...?

No. There were no what-ifs. There were no miracles. He was what he was. A man made bitter, a man whose soul had been pulled away from him. There was no mixing him with Eve, no combining fire and water. That's what they were. As different as fire and water. Light and dark. He had no right to complicate her life by letting her know he loved her. She deserved someone fresh, someone as idealistic as she was. She didn't need him messing up her life.

He turned away from her and stared into the fire again. He had no idea how much time had passed. Finally rousing himself, he went to the bedroom to check on Chester.

Whiskey raised his head as Luke entered the room. Then, satisfied that it was only Luke, he let it drop again on his huge paws. The dog yawned.

Luke waved a dismissing hand at him. "Go back to sleep, dog. You've done your bit," he muttered.

The children were still asleep, huddled together. It had been a scare for them, he thought, one they seemed to have weathered rather well.

Weather. Since the storm had abated yesterday, with any luck he'd be able to reach someone by dawn. By this time tomorrow night, they'd be gone from his life. The cabin would be his again. Peace would be his again. That the thought seemed to add to the emptiness he was feeling only annoyed him. He turned his attention to the old man on the bed.

Chester's eyes were open, and his head was turned in Luke's direction. The old man had been watching him all this time.

"Come to see if the old bird is still alive?" Chester asked.

The deep, raspy voice was weak, but his eyes were clear and at that point Luke knew Chester was going to make it. Relief flooded through him in a sudden, renewed wave. Everything about this family involved feelings he hadn't used in such a long time, he mused. These people forced him to think about emotional baggage that he'd left packed and in the depths of the dark closet of his soul two years ago.

Luke wanted to damn them all for what they had done to him. Wanted to but couldn't. Because for the first time in two years, he felt alive. Really alive.

Luke sat down gingerly on the corner of the bed and laid one booted ankle across his thigh. "I didn't want to put in all that work and have it wasted."

"I see," Chester said.

Did he? Somehow Luke had a feeling he did, but he kept his thoughts to himself, anyway. "Eve would never forgive me if I let you slip away now."

Luke could tell it was an effort for the old man to raise one brow. But he did, and his look probed right into Luke. "And that's important to you, is it?"

"What?" Luke asked evasively. He knew what Chester was driving at. "Not letting you die?"

"No," Chester whispered. "Eve's forgiveness."

Luke felt caught again, like a germ beneath a microscope. He shrugged noncommittally. But Chester's eyes wouldn't let him get away with it.

The whole family had X-ray vision, Luke thought. "Yes." He rose. "Look, you'd better get some rest."

Chester managed to grasp Luke's wrist as he began to move away. For a man who had been on the verge of death such a short while ago, Luke thought, his grip was surprisingly strong. It was a good sign. He looked down at Chester's face, waiting.

"Don't go. I feel like talking."

He didn't want Chester to sap his energy. "I don't think—"

Chester moved his head from side to side slightly. "I'm not going to die, boy. Not yet. But I need to talk. To hear the sound of my own voice. Understand?"

Luke understood. He sat down again.

"I want to thank you for what you did."

Luke shrugged off the old man's thanks. "I would have done it for anyone." He didn't want to be thanked, didn't want bonds between him and these people. It would make the parting that much harder.

"I know." Chester uttered the words firmly.

Luke looked at the man's stubbled face and saw that he was still clear-eyed, lucid. Chester, like Eve, believed in goodness, Luke realized. They hadn't seen the worst side of life, the way he had.

"But it was me you did it for, and I'm grateful."

Luke nodded, wanting the words to pass. For a moment there was silence between them. In the background, he heard the soft, easy breathing of the children as they slept. It was a peaceful sound. A sound he could get used to. He was torturing himself. Why? Was he hoping that if he kept turning the problem around and around, eventually he'd find a side he had missed before? A side that could give him the answer he wanted?

The bedroom felt cold. Luke rose from the bed and put more wood on the dying fire. He stood there, his hands against the top of the fireplace, lost in thought.

"She loves you, boy."

Luke jerked his head around and stared at Chester. "She doesn't *know* me," he insisted. He didn't want the burden of her love. His own feelings for her were hard enough to cope with without the added complication of her love.

The lips beneath the old man's drooping mustache spread weakly in a half smile. "She doesn't know details, but she knows you."

Someone had to listen to reason here, Luke thought in desperation. He didn't want her loving him, couldn't accept it. He didn't have anything nearly as pure to offer her in return. He'd counted on Chester to talk some sense into her. Instead the man sounded as if he gave his blessings.

Luke crossed back to the bed. "This clairvoyance that you and Eve think you have—" he began, annoyed.

But Chester wouldn't be stopped. "Eve feels for people, boy. She makes judgments and sticks by them. She has a way of being right. I don't know. Maybe people just try to live up to what she sees in them."

"Yeah, maybe." But he couldn't.

"She comes on strong."

Luke laughed shortly, fragments of the past few days returning to him. "Tell me about it."

"But she's been hurt. Hurt badly." Luke looked at Chester. They understood each other very well. "I don't want to see her disappointed."

"She won't be." By tonight she'd be gone, he told himself. And she'd never see him again. "Now you get some sleep," he told Chester gruffly.

But Chester had already drifted off.

The old man's words reinforced Luke's decision. He wasn't the one for her, much as he wanted to be. He didn't have it in him to try the way she'd want him to. Up here, for a few days, he had stolen a piece of paradise. But that was all. And it was over. Out in the real world, paradise didn't exist. He knew that. He'd just forgotten for a little while. He had to let Eve go, for her own good, no matter how much he wanted her.

He had to remember that she would be gone soon. He had to gather the fragments of his life and make the best of it.

Luke walked over to his desk and the shortwave radio, spurred on by new determination.

That was how she found him.

Eve woke with a start, the events of the past few hours flooding into her mind in a jumble. She sat up, feeling shaky. The blanket fell away from her. She looked down at it in bewildered surprise. The last she remembered she'd been sitting on the rocker. Luke had carried her in here and covered her. Even in her agitated state, she found that the thought brought a wave of tenderness with it. She looked at him now, his profile all rigid lines and planes, his dark hair falling into his face as he bent over the radio. God, she loved him.

"How's Chester?" she asked.

He turned. He'd gotten used to the sound of her voice, he realized. How empty his life was going to seem without it. "He's mending."

Eve closed her eyes for a moment and sighed. "Thank God."

"If you want to."

The bitterness in his voice was so obvious. She opened her eyes. How could she strip him of his bitterness? It was eating away his soul. After last night, she had hoped that the worst of the battle was over. Now she wasn't so sure. "Luke—" she shook her head "—what am I going to do with you?"

"Nothing."

The single word echoed in the room. The barriers were up again, she thought. Why? They'd been through so much together these past few days. Why was he shutting her out again? Did he regret having shared himself with her?

Of course he did, she told herself. Why else would he sound the way he does? Nobody ever said this was going to be easy. But then, something worth having was worth fighting for. And Luke was worth having.

She brought her knees up to her chest and wound her arms around them, resting her head on the top. "You're pushing me away again," she said quietly.

"I never stopped." The words cost him, but he wouldn't let her see. He kept his eyes on the radio.

"You don't lie very well." She felt tears welling up. Having been through so much, she didn't feel emotionally equipped for another battle.

He ignored her words. "I think I'm getting something."

She rose to her knees on the sofa. The faint squawk faded again. "Are you sure that thing works?" She couldn't think of anything else to say. Not aloud. She wanted to ask him to hold her, to stop fighting her this way. They needed each other. Couldn't he see that?

"It did before you came here," he said, purposely keeping his voice harsh.

"Am I to blame for that, too?"

He glanced at her darkly. He knew he needed to drive her away. He couldn't let himself think of how much the act hurt him. "You're to blame for a lot of things."

His words stabbed her. She raised her chin defiantly. "If it's making you finally open up and feel again, I'm not sorry."

He wanted to go to her, to tell her not to look so hurt. "Some things, Eve, are best left alone."

There was another squawk. This time they heard a faint voice. Luke tried to amplify the power but failed.

"Things," she told him, "not people." She went over to him and tried to make him look at her. His eyes were on her face, but he wasn't seeing her, she thought desperately. He was closing up. She wanted to shake him, to make him stop. "Luke, you're still young. You've got an education. You can start over. Lots of men do it. Why don't you give life another chance?" *Please? For me?* her soul whispered.

His expression never changed. He wouldn't let her see how her words affected him. "Because I don't want to. I like my life here," he said in a brittle voice. "I like my solitude. It's been an interesting interlude, but I want my life to get back to normal. That means I want to be alone."

"No you *don't*," she insisted, her heart breaking.

"What do you do when you're not rearranging people's lives?" His voice had almost a disinterested quality to it. For one split second she thought she hated him. But then she knew she didn't.

"I'm a modeling agency coordinator."

"You should have been a lawyer. You badger like one."

"I don't badger," she insisted. "I cajole."

"You nag, lady." The words were cold, hard. He'd meant them to be so. He *had* to push her back—before he broke and took her into his arms, before he begged her to be part of his life forever even though he had no right to. "Now go back to sleep and leave me to my work," he instructed her curtly. "With any luck I'll have you down the mountain by noon, and you people can have yourselves that Christmas Eve that's so important to you."

Christmas Eve isn't important to me. *You* are, she averred silently, retreating to the sofa.

Dammit, Eve, I'm doing it for your own good. Can't you see that? Just go back and leave me alone before I break down and beg you to stay, he thought miserably.

They fell into a painful silence. Eve told herself she didn't believe him, didn't believe he preferred his solitude to her. But as she lay there, she didn't know if she was merely fooling herself or not.

Could she have been so wrong about him? Could she have fabricated everything, seen only what she wanted to see?

She honestly didn't know.

She closed her eyes for a moment and opened them again when she heard Luke talking excitedly. The fire in the fireplace was dying out. There was light in the cabin. Daylight. It was morning. She glanced at her wristwatch. She'd been asleep for three hours. Her gaze returned to the dark figure at the desk.

Luke looked as if he hadn't slept at all. He was still sitting where she had left him. Except that he was talking now—talking to someone on the radio! Excitement and dread filled her in equal shares. It was over! They'd be rescued. Chester could get to a hospital; the children would have their Christmas.

And she? What would she have? An ache that would last her the rest of her life, she thought, trying to put on a brave face. She tucked her hair behind her ear as she sat up slowly. She had all but begged him last night, and he had turned from her. She had gone as far as she could, bared her soul as much as she dared. The rest was up to him. And he didn't want to stretch the distance, didn't want to close that small gap between them.

The gap might as well have been a deep chasm.

"Yes, yes, I read you," Luke was saying urgently. "Loud and clear, for a change."

"Have you seen anything of some holiday hikers?" a crackling voice asked on the other end. "A woman, an older man and two children. They were reported missing four days ago by a group of campers. The storm kept us from making a search until yesterday, and so far we haven't found a trace of them—''

"Yes, Steve, they're here," Luke interrupted impatiently. "They're okay—"

That was a matter of opinion, Eve thought wryly as she came forward to listen.

He turned slightly in his chair, sensing her nearness. He banked down his emotions and went on talking. "Except for the old man. He's had a mild heart attack. He needs proper medical attention. How soon can you be out here? The pass was still snowed in yesterday afternoon."

"I can have the chopper there in half an hour."

Half an hour, Eve thought. Half an hour to get ready, to bid the rest of her life goodbye. Her throat constricted as she tried to swallow back tears.

Luke glanced at her, his face expressionless. "I'd say they'll be ready to leave by then."

"Terrific. Over and out," Steve replied.

Luke snapped off the radio. "Well, you'll be getting your Christmas Eve, just like the kids wanted," he said, pushing himself away from the desk.

"Right." How she succeeded in keeping the quaver out of her voice, she had no idea. Probably pride. Except that she didn't want to have any pride, not with him. She wanted to shake him and tell him to ask her to stay. Chester could be flown out, but there was no reason that they had to go, too, once she'd seen him properly taken care of in a hospital. The tree was here, decorated by them, and meant more than any tree she'd ever had. Gifts didn't matter. The gift of love was all there really was, and that would be here.

No, it wouldn't, she told herself. She was creating it, just as she must have created a lot of things over the years. He was right; she was too much of a dreamer. And dreamers, sooner or later, had to wake up.

"I'd better get the children ready." Her voice was hollow, empty.

"Need any help?" he offered.

He sounded almost cheerful. He was glad to see them go, so why was she trying to tell herself otherwise? "No, you've done enough already," she assured him.

Eve's voice, stiff and formal, sounded unlike anything he had heard from her. I'm sorry if I'm hurting you Eve, but this hurt is a lot less than anything you'll have to endure later, I promise you.

"Want any coffee?" he called after her, compelled to say something.

"No, I'm sure they'll have plenty at the ranger station," she answered quietly as she walked into the bedroom.

She didn't trust herself to say anything more, or even to turn around and look at him. If she concentrated very hard on everyone else, she told herself, she wouldn't notice how her heart was breaking.

Eve walked into the doorway. Kristin was still sleeping, but Alex was sitting up and rubbing his eyes. "Guess what, everyone!" she announced in a light, cheery voice that echoed back into the other room. "Luke got through to the ranger station. We're going home today."

She was going to be all right, Luke decided as he walked off to the kitchenette to make himself a strong cup of coffee.

Chapter Twelve

It was all going much too quickly, Eve thought. She didn't even have time to draw a breath. Everyone, even the dog, seemed to be moving at once.

Everyone but Luke.

There was noise and confusion all around her, and she knew it was her state of mind and not what was happening that made her feel so disoriented. There was precious little to get ready. All they had to take with them were the clothes on their backs. There was nothing to pack, nothing to do once the children were dressed.

The ache inside her kept throbbing, searching for some sort of release.

She wasn't going to cry, she swore to herself. She'd wait until everything was settled, until Chester was flown in to the hospital and the children were safe in their rooms, before she'd let out this fierce pain. She couldn't relinquish her control, couldn't give in to herself now. Not yet.

"Luke Randall, Luke Randall, did you really talk to a ranger?" Alex asked excitedly, calling from the bedroom as Luke drifted into view, holding his coffee mug. Alex darted away from his mother and rushed out to join him.

Luke took a long draft of steaming coffee before he answered. When he did, his voice was light. He smiled at Alex. "As far as I know he's a ranger."

Kristin was quick to position herself on Luke's other side. "And are they really coming for us?" she asked.

He looked down at the girl's eager face. Eve must have looked like that at her age. Damn, he had to stop doing that.

Why? he asked himself. They'd be gone soon enough, and then there would be no faces to haunt him. None but in his mind. "That's what your mother said, isn't it?" he asked. He ran his hand over Kristin's hair.

Eve caught sight of the tender gesture, and her heart quickened.

"Yes, but—" Kristin was saying.

"Well, you should know by now that your mother doesn't lie."

"That's right. I don't."

There was a sad sort of smile on Eve's lips that cut right through him. Their glances met and held for a moment, mingling like a physical caress before Luke looked back down at Kristin.

"Is he coming with reindeer, like Santa Clause?" Alex asked.

Kristin jabbed her brother in the ribs. "Reindeer can't get through the pass," she said in disgust. "It's snowed in, remember?"

"Flying reindeer could," Alex insisted. He looked to Luke for support.

"Well, you've got the flying part right, Alex," Luke told him. "He's coming to get you by helicopter."

"A real helicopter?" Alex looked as if his eyes were going to fall out of his head, and Luke laughed despite himself. With the laughter came a deep pang. He was going to miss *all* of them.

"A real helicopter," he confirmed. He put down his mug on the table. Suddenly he had no taste for coffee.

"Oh, boy. Kristin, they're coming in a real heli—"

"I heard, I heard," Kristin said, trying not to act excited. But her eyes gave her away.

Outside the cabin was a low, rhythmic noise that got louder as it drew near.

"There's your helicopter now, Alex," Eve said in answer to his questioning look.

Alex ran out without wasting another word. Kristin wasn't far behind.

"Take your jackets!" Eve called after them. The children rushed back, each grabbing a parka, then ran out again.

"I guess they're pretty excited about leaving here," Luke was forced to comment. He couldn't endure the stillness between them.

So what are you going to do later? his mind demanded.

"They're excited about a helicopter ride," Eve corrected him. "I think that all in all they rather liked it here. It was an adventure for them." She looked at

Luke significantly. "For all of us." Dammit, *say* something, she told him silently. Ask me to stay. Give me a sign that I wasn't hallucinating about what was happening between us.

"I'd better go talk to the ranger," Luke muttered as he walked out.

He thought he heard her mumble, "Sure, run," but he continued walking out.

The tall, thin man flanked by Kristin and Alex nodded at Luke as he came out. "They certainly don't seem any the worse for wear," Steve commented. Luke held the door wide open and watched as Steve entered the cabin, followed by Alex and Kristin.

Luke almost envied the ranger the instant camaraderie that seemed to spring up between him and the children. He should be relieved, grateful that they were finally leaving, that he could try to put his life back together again. Instead he was envious of the very man who was rescuing him from this brood's demands on his pantry supply, his time, his emotions.

Luke pushed his thoughts aside and concentrated on helping Steve get Chester comfortably situated in the helicopter.

Once that was accomplished, the rest was easy, or so he told himself. The children bounded on to the helicopter, looking for all the world as if they were off on a new ride at Disneyland. Whiskey, however, was harder to persuade that climbing aboard the helicopter was a good idea. Finally Luke had to lift him into the chopper.

"What does this animal eat?" he muttered at Eve, groaning with exertion as he hefted the dog.

"Scraps," she answered. "Remember?"

Yes, he remembered. He'd remember a lot of things for a long, long time. He wished he wouldn't. "Scraps never felt like this." He exhaled loudly, trying to regulate his breathing. Steve took care of strapping a howling Whiskey in.

"That only leaves you," Steve said, turning to look down at Eve. He extended his hand to her.

"Yes, that only leaves me," she said softly. She looked at Luke hopefully.

"Well, take care of yourself," Luke said distantly.

"Right, sure. You too." Eve turned and took Steve's hand and pulled herself up into the interior of the helicopter.

The wind picked up again and sliced across her face, but she barely felt it. Something else was slicing against her heart a lot harder.

You have to say *something* she told herself. "Luke, I—"

But it was too late. Steve had started the helicopter blades whirling, and the noise drowned out everything else. Besides, Luke was already retreating.

And then he turned and walked away, not even waiting to see them take off.

He didn't care, Eve thought angrily. It was all in her head the whole time.

She faced forward and looked at the approaching sky as the helicopter took off.

It seemed so empty now, Luke thought as he glanced around the cabin the next day. It was at the same time too large and empty and too confining. Echoes of voices seemed to be in every corner, haunting him. He hadn't watched them take off yesterday, hadn't been able to face that final sight. Instead, he'd walked back into the cabin and gotten in contact with Bruce, who had been relieved to hear from him. The reports Luke had taken were duly noted and received.

He'd done everything he could think of in the past twenty-four hours to get his mind off Eve. He had failed. Wandering around the cabin, he couldn't find a place for himself. The cabin felt like a shoe that had once been comfortable but now had been outgrown.

"The peace and quiet is too much for you Randall. Stop feeling sorry for yourself and get to work."

With that, he shrugged into his jacket and walked to the door. He had to check the equipment today. After all, that was what he was supposed to do, right?

He realized he was holding the door open, waiting for Eve to join him. Annoying habits formed quickly, he thought angrily, slamming the door behind him.

He trudged off into the snow, calling himself several kinds of a fool.

He missed her company. He missed her smell. The way her laughter seemed to fill the air. Everything seemed different.

It'll be all right, he thought angrily. It'll just take time, that's all.

He knew he was lying.

But he repeated the lie over and over again as he faithfully transcribed the readings into his notebook, forcing his mind to take a familiar route. His self-control lasted long enough for him to write down the last notation. And even that had been difficult. His mind kept wandering. He kept remembering bits and pieces of the past four days, examining them like precious jewels, taking them out one by one and going over them until they gleamed in his mind's eye.

Things *weren't* going to go back to normal. He'd changed. She had made him change, had made him reassess his life, his reasons for seeking this retreat. He realized that just as she had said, the man who had lived here for the past two years, severed from the world, wasn't the real Luke Randall. The past two years had been a form of self-preservation. If he had stayed in Philadelphia, he would have really changed, sunk to the lows he feared awaited him. His bitterness would have eaten away at him until there was nothing left. Coming out here had actually been a way of preserving his inner self until it was strong enough to thrive on its own. To this end, he'd built a shell around himself, a cocoon, isolating himself from everything and everyone. But the cocoon in itself had almost overpowered him. He couldn't reemerge by himself. He'd needed help. He'd needed Eve to make him whole again.

He slammed his notebook shut. "You big idiot, you let her go. The best damned thing that ever happened to you and you had to go on wearing your hair shirt like some martyr, beating your chest and saying that you were damned. Well, you will be, if you don't do something about getting her back."

Luke locked the cabin door, making his declaration to the air, to the snow on the ground and to a foraging rabbit. "She's right. I've been running from me, and I've got to take me along wherever I go. Like San Diego."

The name of the city made him smile for the first time that day. Really smile. He was going to go after her. He had no idea where she lived, but he knew her name. How large was San Diego? Even if it were the largest city in the world, he'd find her. He'd have to. He wasn't going to lose his soul twice.

With determined steps, his mind racing ahead to make plans, he strode back to his cabin. He'd have to get in contact with the ranger station again. He knew Steve wouldn't be thrilled about flying back up here, but this was an emergency. He *had* to get to San Diego. Wait, he told himself. Maybe she was still at the lodge—or at the hospital. Steve might know. Even if he didn't, Luke wasn't going to let that stop him. Wherever she was—the lodge, San Diego, Timbuktu—he was going to find her.

The thought made his breath quicken. He'd throw some things together into a duffel bag and camp out in *her* house. He grinned at the thought. Turnabout was fair play. And for the first time in a long time, he decided that maybe life did play fair once in a while. Maybe it did try to balance the odds, even though he hadn't realized it at the time.

Eve walked out of the hospital room and into the corridor. Alex and Kristin jumped up from the bench where they had been sitting.

"Is he going to be all right, Mom?" Kristin asked, anxiously searching her mother's face.

Eve put an arm around each child and hugged them. Hard. "He's going to be fine." She took a deep breath and then let it out slowly. She felt as if she'd been up for a hundred hours. But the worst was over, at least as far as Chester was concerned.

She immediately felt guilty at being so selfish. Chester was going to live. That should be enough of a miracle for her.

Eve released her hold on the children and took each by the hand. "Say, how about getting something to eat? I hear the food's not too bad in the cafeteria."

"Okay," Alex said.

"I'm not very hungry." Kristin looked over her shoulder at the closed door.

Eve knew what her daughter was thinking. "He's fine, really. He's even grumbling."

Kristin slowly nodded her assent. "Maybe I could eat."

"Sure you could," Eve said encouragingly. As long as I keep thinking about the children and Chester, I won't think about the pain in my heart. They started to walk down the corridor, but stopped short.

There, walking toward them, was Luke. She was too stunned to speak.

Luke halted a few feet away from them. He didn't know why, but he was suddenly afraid to close the final gap physically. His throat felt dry. "How's Chester?" he managed to get out.

"He's doing wonderfully. So well, in fact, that the doctors are amazed. They say you saved his life. Uncle Chester certainly seems to think so." She let her gaze rake over him. What was he doing here? It couldn't be what she was thinking.

"And the dog?"

"He developed a rapport with the ranger, so we let him stay there while Steve flew us up to the hospital."

We're talking like strangers, Luke thought. But at least we're talking.

Eve couldn't make herself believe that he was actually here. She felt as if she were watching everything in slow motion. She proceeded carefully. "What are you doing here?"

Luke felt unsure of himself, like a teenager all over again. "I've been doing some thinking." Why were the words so damn hard to get out? he wondered. Because, he knew, he was afraid of her answer.

"And?" Eve held her breath. He was *here*. Yes, Virginia, there *is* a Santa Claus.

"And..." He drew a breath. "I decided you were right. Christmas Eve is for families," he continued, his voice hardly rising above a whisper. He struggled to maintain his calm appearance.

"I'll go along with that," she said. "That still doesn't explain what you're doing here." She wasn't going to let herself think about the possibilities, wasn't going to grab at any false hopes.

He saw that the children were watching him with wide eyes, almost like the first time. Here goes, Luke thought, plunging forward. "I decided that I'm going to be part of your family—whether you like it or not."

"And I have no say in the matter?" Eve tried hard to hide the smile that was growing within her. Warmth began to seep through her body.

"None," he said firmly, never taking his eyes from hers.

Eve moved toward him slowly, treading as if the ground would open up and swallow her before she reached him. "That's your final decision?"

"My final decision." He watched her until she stopped next to him. The children suddenly came to life and jumped up eagerly, each taking a side around him. "So what's your answer?" he asked.

A smile crinkled her eyes as she said, "I thought it didn't matter."

Luke started to feel relief budding within him. "It doesn't. Still, it would be nice for the children to hear."

The smile spread over her face. "The children." She nodded knowingly. "I like it. I like it just fine."

Luke let go of the breath he'd been holding. "Oh, there's just one more thing."

"Oh?"

"I'd like to make it legal."

Kristin stared up at him, confused. "Aren't you a little old to be adopted?" Alex giggled.

Luke wove his fingers through Eve's, his eyes never leaving her face. "I wasn't quite thinking of adoption, Kristin. I was thinking of asking your mother to marry me." He looked down at the little girl at his side. "Think she'll go for it?"

Kristin nodded vigorously.

"How about it, Eve?" Luke asked. "Want to add a rehabilitated scalp to your belt?"

"I don't collect scalps."

"What do you collect?"

She smiled at him warmly. "Love."

"You've already got mine," he told her, taking her into his arms. "Forever and always. Now, let's go tell that cantankerous uncle of yours he's just gotten himself a new nephew-in-law." He moved to open the door of the hospital room, then took another look at Eve's upturned face. He grinned. "Well, maybe in a few minutes."

It was a little hard kissing Eve while two children hugged him, but he managed. And he knew that he was going to go on managing just fine from this day forward.

* * * * *

Silhouette Special Edition

THE O'HURLEYS! MADDY'S STORY

from
Nora Roberts

Dance To The Piper

Available July 1988

The second in an exciting new series about the lives and
loves of triplet sisters—

If *The Last Honest Woman* (SE #451) captured your
heart in May, you're sure to want to read about Maddy
and Chantel, Abby's two sisters.

In *Dance to the Piper* (SE #463), it takes some very
fancy footwork to get reserved recording mogul Reed
Valentine dancing to effervescent Maddy's tune....

Then, in *Skin Deep* (SE #475), find out what kind of
heat it takes to melt the glamorous Chantel's icy heart.
Available in September.

THE O'HURLEYS!

**Join the excitement of
Silhouette Special Editions.**

Silhouette ❧ _Romance_

COMING NEXT MONTH

#592 JUSTIN—Diana Palmer
Book 2 in the LONG, TALL TEXANS Trilogy!
Rugged cowboy Justin Ballenger was the man of Shelby Jacobs's dreams, but
years ago circumstances had ended their engagement, leaving Justin
brokenhearted and bitter. Could Shelby convince him she'd never stopped
loving him?

#593 SHERLOCK'S HOME—Sharon De Vita
Arrogant detective Mike Ryce wanted to be little T. C. Sherlock's foster father,
but welfare agent Wilhelmina Walker thought he was wrong for the job. So why
was Mike gaining custody of her heart?

#594 FINISHING TOUCH—Jane Bierce
Clay Dowling's corporation was threatening to destroy Rose Davis's cozy
cottage. She had to fight him, but would she lose her heart to his Southern
charm before she won the war?

#595 THE LADYBUG LADY—Pamela Toth
From the moment Cassie Culpepper sprayed Jack Hoffman with the garden
hose to keep him from killing her ladybugs, she'd captured his attention. Now
he wanted the lovely Ladybug Lady to fly—straight to _his_ home....

#596 A NIGHT OF PASSION—Lucy Gordon
The greatest joy in Veronica Grant's life had begun with one night of passion in
Jordan Cavendish's arms. But she'd kept their child a secret, and now she and
her daughter desperately needed Jordan's help....

#597 THE KISS OF A STRANGER—Brittany Young
In the Scottish Highlands, Clarissa Michaels met James Maxwell, the man who
had claimed her heart with one kiss. But Clarissa's life was in danger while she
stayed in James's ancestral castle. Had destiny brought them together only to
tear them apart?

AVAILABLE THIS MONTH:

Silhouette Intimate Moments

At Dodd Memorial Hospital, Love is the Best Medicine

When temperatures are rising and pulses are racing, Dodd Memorial Hospital is the place to be. Every doctor, nurse and patient is a heart specialist, and their favorite prescription is a little romance. This month, finish Lucy Hamilton's Dodd Memorial Hospital Trilogy with HEARTBEATS, IM #245.

Nurse Vanessa Rice thought police sergeant Clay Williams was the most annoying man she knew. Then he showed up at Dodd Memorial with a gunshot wound, and the least she could do was be friends with him—if he'd let her. But Clay was interested in something more, and Vanessa didn't want that kind of commitment. She had a career that was important to her, and there was no room in her life for any man. But Clay was determined to show her that they could have a future together—and that there are times when the patient knows best.
